Dawn smoothed her hair and felt something sticky on her fingers. She looked at them. They were covered in red lipstick. She ran to the vanity mirror. Her flaxen hair had lipstick streaks everywhere.

Maybe she could at least use a pumice stone to remove the lipstick from her fingers. The stone had a strange green cast to it — almost glowing. Whatever. She buffed away at the tips of her fingers, where the lipstick was worst.

Dawn smiled. The lipstick was disappearing.

Then she gasped.

Because the tips of her fingers were disappearing, too.

SMALLVILLE™

Arrival #1

See No Evil #2

Pet Peeve #3, arriving December 2002

Flight #4, arriving February 2003

See No Evil

SMALLVILLE™

See No Evil

Cherie Bennett and Jeff Gottesfeld

Superman created by
Jerry Siegel and Joe Shuster

Little, Brown and Company
BOSTON NEW YORK LONDON

First Edition

ISBN 0-316-17301-0
LCCN 2002103574

10 9 8 7 6 5 4 3 2 1

Q-BF

Printed in the United States of America

CHAPTER 1

Amidst the teen chaos that was the end of the day at Smallville High School, Clark Kent stood at his locker and spun the combination. As usual, his locker was stuck. He nonchalantly tapped the metal door with his forefinger, using the slightest possible effort. It popped open like a jack-in-the-box.

Lucky they gave the sticky one to the kid with the secret superstrength, Clark thought, as he pulled out the books he needed for homework.

"Yo, Clark!"

His best friend, Pete Ross, was waving to him from the other side of the crowded hallway. Pete had to jump up a little to be seen. They'd been friends forever, and Clark knew how much it galled Pete that Clark had gone through a major growth spurt in the past year and Pete, well . . . hadn't.

"What's up?" Clark asked, when Pete had dodged his way through the teeming masses.

Peter held up the thick textbook he was carrying. "Definitely not my grade in math. How about if we head over to the Beanery and study for the quiz? If you can get chapter ten through my head, the double caramel lattes are on me."

Clark closed his locker and shot Pete a bemused look. "You might want to bone up on chapters one through nine first. And maybe cut down a little on the caffeine intake."

"Witty. Remind me to laugh when I'm not sweating out the possibility of a big fat F, which will cause my parentals to hold me hostage until further notice. I'm desperate for a speed-tutor and you're my man. Deal?"

"Can't," Clark said, as they started down the hall. "I told Lana I'd meet her in the theater. She's working on the school play."

"Yeah, a date with Lana Lang definitely trumps math and a coffee buzz," Pete acknowledged.

"It's not a *date*. She said some guys bailed on the cast and asked if I'd help out."

Pete shrugged. "Take it from me, Clark. When it comes to women, it's all about the geographical imperative. Proximity is key. You'll be hanging with Lana at play practice while Whitney Fordman, her so-called boyfriend, is elsewhere. Lana will finally see you for the stud you are. He's out, you're in, life is sweet, that about covers it."

Clark looked dubious. "Since when do you know so much about women?"

"It's like this." Pete put his hand on his friend's shoulder. "I may suck at anything requiring a calculator, but ladies are my long suit. And I guarantee *that* knowledge will get me a lot farther than non-acute angles." He pulled out his shades and slipped them on. "*Asta-lou*-later, my man."

Clark laughed. They reached the front doors, and Pete stepped out into the afternoon sunshine. A thought struck Clark as he watched his friend walk away:

If Pete Ross is such an expert on women, why doesn't he have a girlfriend?

ꕥ ꕥ ꕥ ꕥ

Clark paused outside the auditorium long enough to gaze at the large poster display for Smallville High's production of *Cyrano de Bergerac.* Led by longtime drama teacher Mr. Gullet, the school was well-known for putting on excellent student productions. Clark had seen many of them with his parents. He remembered his first play vividly, even though he'd been only eight. *Peter Pan.* The actor playing Peter had "flown" across the stage with the aid of nearly invisible slender wires.

To young Clark, it had seemed as if Peter Pan were really flying. But since heights made him queasy even then, just watching the actor soar had made him feel sick to his stomach.

Great memory to start my theatrical career, Clark thought wryly, as he stepped into the auditorium.

It was a beehive of activity. On one side of the stage, a dozen kids were running lines. On the opposite side, kids were "dueling" with swords —

reviewing their fight choreography under Mr. Gullet's guidance. Meanwhile, six students hammered away on the set, building a balcony, while two others carried in a ladder that evidently would lead up to it.

"Costume parade in ten minutes, people!" Carrie Levin, the stage manager, bellowed over the din. She ducked as one of the duelers almost ran into her. "Jeremy, would you chill with that sword? I'd like to live until opening night."

All Clark could think was: *What the heck am I doing here?*

Well, he knew the answer to that one. Two words: Lana Lang. Clark caught sight of her up onstage, part of the stage crew. Even when she was in grungy jeans and a T-shirt, with a sawdust smudge on her cheek, Clark found Lana unspeakably beautiful.

With her glossy raven hair and delicate features, any guy would have said she was great-looking. But for Clark, it was so much more, beyond words. Which was a good thing, since when he was around her, too often he felt as if he could barely speak.

And when she wears that necklace with the green meteor chip in it, I definitely feel like I can't speak. In fact, I can barely stand up.

Lana and her aunt lived next door to the Kent farm (if you didn't count a lot of farmland in between). Yet for the longest time, it had seemed to Clark as if the two of them were a million miles apart. The truth was, he'd been in love with her ever since he'd removed a bee stinger from her foot on the playground in kindergarten. Not that he'd ever told her he loved her, of course.

Lately, he and Lana had become friends. Maybe more than friends. But Lana had a boyfriend, senior Whitney Fordman. And Clark had, well, secrets. Minor stuff. Like superpowers. Like having landed on earth in a spaceship when he was three, during the same meteor shower that had killed Lana's parents. Little secrets like that.

Up onstage, Lana looked up from her hammering, noticed Clark, and grinned. Even from the rear of the two-hundred-seat theater, Clark could feel the radiance of that smile. He headed down the aisle and bounded up to the stage.

"Clark! I'm glad you came," Lana said, putting the hammer back in the toolbox. "To be honest, I wasn't sure you would."

"Hey, wouldn't miss it."

She laughed. "Liar."

He shrugged sheepishly. "Well, I'll give it my best shot. By the way, what's a costume parade?"

"It's where everyone in the cast tries on their costumes and models them for Mr. Gullet so he can decide if anything needs changing. You know Jenni Favor from math class?"

Clark nodded. "The shy girl with the freckles, right?"

"Right. She's a demon with needle and thread. She made most of the —"

"Coming through, coming through!" Two burly guys lugged a heavy, old-fashioned couch toward Clark and Lana. "C'mon, move it."

Clark edged out of the way, knowing that he could hoist both couch *and* guys without cracking a sweat. Not that anyone knew about that except his parents. Not that he could ever tell anyone. Ever. *Ever* ever.

Clark pushed his hands into the pockets of his jeans. "So, it's kind of . . . disorganized."

"I know it looks like that at the moment, but I assure you there's a method to the madness." Lana craned around, looking for the drama teacher, who was no longer on the stage. "Mr. Gullet is going to be so happy to see you. That is, if I can find him."

A buzz of trepidation flittered through Clark. "I have zero experience at this, Lana. I doubt that I have any talent."

Lana tapped one finger against her lips. "For some reason, Clark, I have a feeling you're going to be a natural."

"Why's that?"

She cocked her head contemplatively. "I don't know, exactly. It's just that I get this feeling that you could pretend to be someone you're not and fool all of the people, all of the time."

Clark flushed. This remark was a little too close to home. He tried to joke his way out of it. "Gee, maybe I have a future in politics, then."

Lana smiled, but her eyes were serious. "Just a feeling. Still waters run deep with you, Clark.

Oh, there's Mr. Gullet." She hurried over to the teacher, who was just offstage, and spoke with him quickly.

Mr. Gullet raised his bushy eyebrows and motioned for Clark to join them. When Clark walked over, he said, "So, Mr. Kent, I understand that you're the super hero who is going to rescue my play."

"Who, me? No, not me," Clark stammered. "I've never even . . . I mean, Lana told me that a couple of actors dropped out, so a small part would be —"

Mr. Gullet held up one hand. "Joking, Mr. Kent. Miss Lang already told me that you've never acted before. Not to worry. I try not to terrorize the neophytes. Congratulations. You are now officially cast as Flunky Number Two."

"Thanks," Clark said. "There's really a part named Flunky Number Two?"

"Rostand, the playwright, wrote in French," Mr. Gullet explained, "so we're at the mercy of translators. You could call yourself Sycophant Number Two, if you prefer."

"I'll stick with Flunky."

The teacher smiled. "Excellent choice. Have a script."

How tough can it be to play Flunky Number Two? Clark thought, as he took the script from Mr. Gullet. *Maybe Pete's right. Working on the play with Lana could be the perfect game plan. I'll probably have a lot of free time since my part is so small. Once the set is done, Lana will have a lot of free time, too. So between her free time and my free time —*

"Mr. Kent?" Mr. Gullet's voice pulled Clark out of his reverie. "Are you with us on earth, or busy planet-hopping?"

"Huh? Oh, sorry, sir. Did you say something?"

"I said that I'd have Flunky Number One show you your blocking — 'blocking' means where you go and when you go there. The two of you stand next to each other in every scene. You can handle that, can't you?"

"Absolutely," Clark assured him.

"Good to know." Mr. Gullet peered deep into the wings. "Mr. Fordman, could you come over here, please?"

Clark's heart sank as Whitney popped up from

behind a flat that had blocked him from view. It had never entered Clark's mind that Whitney, a.k.a. the Jock King of Smallville High, a.k.a. Lana's Significant Other, could possibly be involved in *Cyrano*. From the look on Whitney's face, he was equally surprised — and unhappy — to see Clark.

Mr. Gullet gave instructions, then shooed them away. Whitney reluctantly led Clark across the stage. "Come on, Kent. It's not exactly brain surgery." They reached a half-painted wooden doorway. "This is where we enter at the beginning of scene one. So since when are you interested in theater?"

"Funny, I was going to ask you the same thing."

Whitney shrugged. "Looks good on college applications."

Right, Clark thought. *As if you're not here because of Lana.*

"Anyway," Whitney continued, "when the bugler blows his bugle in act one — that's *if* the kid gets a note out — he's got wicked asthma so you never know — we cross to that flat." Whitney cocked his head toward the back of the stage, where a flat was partially painted an outdoorsy green. "Then, after Cyrano enters, we —"

"Where the hell is Jenni Favor?" a female voice thundered imperiously. The voice belonged to Dawn Mills, reigning queen of the drama department, who had swept onto the stage. Her long golden hair was pinned atop her head. She was clad in a low-cut, emerald green, floor-length gown.

Dawn and her boyfriend, Mike Karn, had the leads in all the school's productions. It was common knowledge that both hoped to study theater at Juilliard in New York after graduation. They were seniors; Clark had never met either of them. But he'd seen Dawn play Kim MacAfee in *Bye Bye Birdie* and Laura in *The Glass Menagerie*. He thought she was incredibly talented. From the audience, her sun-kissed hair and feline eyes had looked stunningly beautiful. Now, though, as she stood center stage and looked around haughtily for Jenni, he could see that there was a nasty sneer to Dawn's thin lips.

"Can you even believe this?" Dawn asked her friends, Missy and Julie. The three of them were usually together, Missy and Julie serving as Dawn's Greek chorus. In the play, they were cast as nuns.

As Missy and Julie shook their heads at the horror of Dawn's plight, little Jenni scurried toward them. "Do you have a problem, Dawn?"

"No, Jenni. You do." Dawn grabbed a handful of green material from the skirt of her gown. "Is this your idea of a joke, or did you actually mean for me to wear this piece of crap?"

Jenni's pale skin went blotchy red. Her freckles stood out like dot-to-dots. "Uh, well, Mr. Gullet told me to go through the costumes that are stored in the scene shop and pick out what I thought would work for you, so since I was already making your other costumes, I thought —"

"Do us all a favor," Dawn snapped. "Don't think. It's not your long suit."

"No kidding," Missy agreed. Julie nodded her agreement.

"Jenni, here's what you need to do." Dawn spoke with deliberate slowness, as if Jenni was just beginning to learn English. "Go find Gullet. Tell him you made a big, fat error. Get the key to the prop-and-costume shop. Bring it to me, so I can find something decent to wear. Think you can handle that?"

"I . . . sure . . . I mean . . ." Jenni backed away from Dawn, then turned and fled.

Dawn looked disgusted. "That's the best Gullet could get for a costume designer? Why am I even still doing plays here?"

Clark, who'd seen this whole exchange, turned to Whitney. "She's got quite the temper."

"Dawn's a brat," Whitney agreed, "of the spoiled, rich variety."

Together, they watched as Dawn's boyfriend, Mike Karn, dressed in his Cyrano outfit but minus the large nose that was Cyrano's signature, came onstage, swept Dawn into his arms, and kissed her as if the whole auditorium had paid a fortune to witness their game of tonsil hockey.

"They're at it again, I see," Lana noted, as she joined Clark and Whitney.

Clark couldn't help staring at the endless liplock. "Don't they come up for air?"

"Not if it keeps people looking at them," Lana said. "And it does. So, how are you guys doing?"

"Fine," Clark and Whitney said, pretty much at the same time.

"Come on, Kent," Whitney said grudgingly. "I'll show you the rest of act one. Your line is 'M'lady.'"

"That's it?" Clark asked. "'M'lady'?"

"You're a flunky, what'd you expect?" Whitney asked. "One more thing, Kent."

"What's that?"

"This one line of yours? Try not to blow it."

Chapter 2

Dawn stomped up to the winding staircase that bisected the ornate front hallway of her palatial home and swept into her elegant, oversized bedroom. She threw herself down on her queen-sized canopy bed, furious over everything that had gone wrong at rehearsal. Why did she have to work with such amateurs?

She couldn't wait until she graduated and left the stupid little burg of Smallville far behind. There was no joy in getting the lead anymore, no satisfaction in being told how wonderful she was in every play. Being the queen-bee actress of Smallville High was so . . . so junior year. It had been exciting then, to know that every guy wanted to date her and every girl wanted to hang out with her. But now even Mike was starting to bore her. She knew she had him wrapped around her perfectly French-manicured little finger. There was no challenge left. She was just marking time.

People told her how lucky she was to work with the great Mr. Gullet. Please. So what if he'd studied at Juilliard himself? That was back when dinosaurs roamed the earth. Besides, if Gullet was really any good, she knew he'd be acting professionally, not directing school plays in the boonies of Kansas.

She flounced over to her vanity table and sat down, staring at her heart-shaped mirror, which was lit by dozens of tiny, recessed, pink light-bulbs. Lifting her hair off her neck, she contemplated her image and tried to decide which Hollywood star she most resembled. Missy said she looked just like Gwyneth Paltrow. Julie insisted she was a dead ringer for Kate Hudson. Each assured her she was more talented than both of those women put together.

"They're right," Dawn told her reflection. She

let her hair cascade over her shoulders and picked up her hairbrush. Idly brushing her hair, she went to the window and gazed out at the backyard. The late afternoon sunlight lit the formal gardens with an ochre glow; one of the gardener's assistants was pruning the shrubbery. Dawn contemplated his rippling muscles. *Hmm. Tasty,* she thought. He looked to be college age. She considered wandering down and flirting a little.

She smoothed her hair and felt something thick and sticky on her fingers. She looked at them. They were covered in red Chanel lipstick. She looked at her hairbrush. The bristles were *scarlet.* She ran to the vanity mirror. Her flaxen hair had lipstick streaks everywhere.

"Tillie," she muttered murderously. Clearly, her bratty little fifth-grader sister had snuck into her room yet again to play with her makeup. Dawn spun around to head for Tillie's room and yelped. She'd stepped on something embedded in one of the heirloom rugs scattered over the burnished floorboards. It was one of Tillie's trademark calling cards — a stone.

Other kids collected Barbies or stuffed animals. Not Tillie. A junior rock hound, she had bookshelves full of rocks and minerals she'd collected from around town. The hobby was bad enough. But Tillie also had the most annoying habit of leaving her stupid rocks all over the house.

Dawn picked up Tillie's stone and fired it at the wastebasket. She missed. When she retrieved it to drop it in the trash, she saw that Tillie had almost-but-not-quite disposed of three broken lipsticks. One of them was the Chanel lipstick that now adorned her hair.

"Oh, Tillie, you are *so* dead," she growled. But before she made her sister's life a living hell, she had to do something about her hair. Washing it took forever. Maybe she could wipe it off. Tentatively, Dawn ran a tissue over a hunk of red-coated hair. But that only seemed to smear the lipstick around.

Arrgh! Maybe she could at least pumice the lipstick off her fingers. She searched for her pumice stone but couldn't find it. The brat had probably added it to her collection. Beyond irritated, Dawn grabbed Tillie's stupid stone out of the trash. It had a strange green cast to it — almost glowing. Whatever. She buffed away at the tips of her fingers, where the lipstick was worst.

Dawn smiled. The lipstick was disappearing.

Then she gasped.

Because the tips of her fingers were disappearing, too.

Chapter 3

Breathless with fear, Dawn ran into her bathroom, stuck her hand under the faucet, and yanked on the water. It ran scalding hot over the place where her fingertips used to be.

As the water gushed into the sink, her fingertips returned to visibility. Dawn sagged against the sink with relief. This was too freaky. Fingers didn't just disappear and reappear. It had to be an optical illusion or something. Didn't it?

She retrieved Tillie's green rock, then sat cross-legged on the edge of the bathtub. Cautiously, she started rubbing the stone against one heel.

A knock at the door interrupted her.

"Go away *now,*" Dawn ordered, knowing it had to be her sister.

"What are you doing?" Tillie called.

"Nothing that concerns you, freak." Dawn kept buffing her heel. She watched in amazement as it disappeared. She worked the stone over the rest of her foot. It disappeared, too.

"Are you doing drugs in there?" Tillie demanded.

"Yes, it's called *rock,*" Dawn replied. "Now go crawl back under yours." She turned on the water and stuck her foot under it. It reappeared. Amazing.

"If you're doing drugs, I'm telling. Do you hear me?" Tillie kicked angrily at the door.

Suddenly, Tillie was no more than an annoying flea. Dawn's mind raced, and a slow smile crawled over her lips. She had just discovered the power to make herself invisible. All she had to do to become visible again was to get wet.

The possibilities were mind-boggling.

Tillie kicked at the door again, harder.

"Oh, Tillie," Dawn sing-songed sweetly. "I'm counting to three. If I open the door and you're still there, I will make you wish you had never been born. One. Two."

Dawn could almost hear her sister considering it, followed by pounding footsteps as Tillie fled. Good. She'd deal with the little cretin later. Dawn turned her attention back to the green stone, and an idea formed in her mind. She said she had wanted a challenge. . . .

Dawn stripped off her clothes and began to pumice the bottom half of her body. Her toes disappeared. Then her feet. Anklcs. Legs. She felt giddy when she looked in the mirror and saw a legless torso. Once the stone reached her hips, the rest of her body — hair included — magically faded away.

Holy sugar on a shingle. She was gone.

Invisible heart pounding, Dawn stepped into the shower. As the water splashed over her, she became visible again. Too cool! There were so many possibilities! She could sneak into teachers' offices and steal tests. Check out hot guys in the locker room. Spy on her boyfriend.

Dawn tilted her head back, reached for her shampoo, and laughed in triumph. She could do anything. And no one could stop her.

It couldn't have happened to a more deserving person.

ꕥ ꕥ ꕥ ꕥ

A box of organic vegetables in hand, Clark jammed his finger against Lex Luthor's doorbell. Lex had a standing order for Kent Farm vegetables, and Clark was making one of his regular deliveries.

Lex opened the door. He was clad in a black warm-up suit; a white towel was draped around his neck. "Clark!" Lex greeted his friend warmly and took the vegetable box. "How is Smallville High's newest thespian?"

Clark was taken aback. "Wait, how do you know about that?"

Instead of answering, Lex smiled and put the vegetables on a marble table. "Come on in. Don't worry about the vegetables. The cook will get them later."

"If I'm interrupting your workout, I can —"

Lex shook his head. "Just finished. Ever try

kickboxing, Clark? You can level an opponent twice your size with one well-placed right foot."

"I'll keep that in mind."

Clark stepped into the cavernous hallway of the Luthor mansion, marveling as he often did at even being there. The two of them met when Clark had saved Lex's life after Lex's car had careened off a bridge. Clark had used superpowers he hadn't even known he'd possessed to rip the top off Lex's car and save him from a watery grave.

That unlikely meeting had led to an unlikely friendship. Five years older than Clark, Lex was the wealthy son of one of the world's great industrialists, Lionel Luthor. Lionel had sent Lex to the best schools and traveled the world with his son. But Clark knew there was no love lost between son and father, which is why Lionel had banished Lex to Smallville, ostensibly to run one of LuthorCorp's fertilizer factories.

And I'm the son of Jonathan and Martha Kent, Clark thought. *We barely make ends meet on a family farm. I've never been farther from Smallville than*

Metropolis. Unless you count that I'm from another planet. My father says Lionel can't be trusted. And now he says the same thing about Lex.

Clark could practically hear his father's voice: "In my experience, the apple doesn't fall far from the tree. I just don't trust him."

Which is so unfair, Clark thought now. *I mean, I don't even know what family tree I'm from. I sure wouldn't want someone judging me because of that.*

"Beverage?" Lex offered when they reached the library. He took two blue bottles of imported water from a small refrigerator and handed one to Clark.

"Thanks." Clark took a swig of water. "So, really, how did you know I was in the school play?"

"When you're underwriting the production, you like to stay on top of things." Lex raised his bottle in a silent toast and then took a sip.

Clark was surprised. "What prompted that?"

"Call it community relations," Lex said. "I'm also donating a new lighting board. The one your school is using must have been manufactured when Rostand wrote *Cyrano*. Good choice of play, incidentally. One of my favorites." Lex sat behind his desk and motioned Clark toward the couch.

"I like the play, too," Clark said, as he took a seat. "I'm just not sure I like being in it."

"But when the fair Miss Lang calls, you answer," Lex said.

"Do you have spies following me or something?"

Lex regarded him with bemusement. "Should I?"

"No," Clark said quickly. "I mean, I'm not all that interesting." He grew uncomfortable under Lex's gaze and went to the window, just for something to do.

"Ever see Gérard Depardieu's *Cyrano?*" Lex asked, swigging again from the bottle. "I'll lend you the DVD, you should watch it sometime. Invite Lana."

Clark turned back to his friend. "I can't. Whitney's —"

"In the play, too. I told you, I know everything. The quarterback is only a minor irritant, Clark. Challenge him to a duel. To the death, if you like. I'll supply the swords."

The twinkle in Lex's eye told Clark he was joking. Mostly.

Clark leaned against the wall. "At least I only have one line. 'M'lady.'"

Lex nodded. "Roxanne's act one entrance."

"Wow, you know the play that well?"

"Does it surprise you?" Lex contemplated the opaque coolness of the blue water bottle. "Cyrano was the greatest swordsman in all of France. Anyway, Clark, *Cyrano* is a classic. Classics are to be cherished. Especially the rare one that is actually decent."

Clark nervously ran a hand through his hair. "Maybe I should be cherishing it from the audience. We did a run-through today. I managed to mess up my one and only line. I guess I have stage fright."

Lex stood. "In that case, Clark, you're doing the right thing. Fears are to be confronted. If you're scared of snakes, make one your pet. Scared of heights? Jump from a plane." A mirthless smile tugged at the corners of his mouth. "I, for example, was once afraid of my father."

"What's the cure for that?" Clark wondered.

"Simple. I beat him at his own game. And then, Clark," Lex said, staring hard into Clark's eyes, "I crush him."

ꕤ ꕤ ꕤ ꕤ

"I hate Dawn, she's a great big yawn, and I wish she'd never been born."

Tillie Mills made up the song as she went along, switching to a hum as she polished her newest rock. It was boring brown, like her boring hair and her boring eyes. Why did Dawn have to get the gold hair and the green eyes and *everything?* No one ever told Tillie she was beautiful or that she was going to be a star.

Sometimes Tillie wondered what it would be like to have a big sister who liked her, took her places, and told her secrets. Fat chance. Dawn hated her. Well, tough titmouse. Tillie hated Dawn right back. She wished her sister would just disappear. That'd be *sweet.*

Fat chance. Dawn liked to be looked at more

than anyone in the world. Tillie set her newest mineral on her shelf. At least rocks didn't call you names and make you feel bad. A hunger pang rumbled through her plump stomach. What did she feel like eating? Peanut butter.

Her mother kept it hidden on a high shelf, because she thought Tillie was too fat. Well, tough titmouse to her, too. In the gleaming, state-of-the-art kitchen, she took out the bread and then scrambled onto the counter so that she could reach the forbidden peanut butter. She nabbed it and jumped down.

Just as Tillie was spooning some superchunky into her mouth, she felt a tap on her shoulder. She turned around.

No one was there.

Huh. Must be her imagination. She dug into the peanut butter jar again.

"Tillie?"

Tillie whipped around. The voice was definitely Dawn's. But Dawn was nowhere in sight. Tillie put down her peanut butter spoon. "Where are you?"

"Wouldn't you like to know?" Dawn's voice

taunted. "Sneaking peanut butter, huh, Miss Piggy? No wonder you're so fat."

"You shut up!" Tillie warned. "I hate you, and when I find you —"

"Ooh, I'm so-o scared," Dawn's voice cooed from the thin air.

"You *should* be scared." Tillie grabbed a butter knife from a drawer and held it high like a weapon. She stalked through the kitchen, expecting her sister to pop out of some hiding place at any minute.

But there was no sign of Dawn. If her sister was hiding, she'd picked a really good hiding place. Just as Tillie turned back to the peanut butter, something knocked the knife from her hand. Invisible arms grabbed her and lifted her into the air.

"No, no-o! Tillie screamed. She struggled, but whatever *thing* was wrestling Tillie carried her over to the sink and turned on the garbage disposal. "No-o! Please, no-o!" Tillie begged, as her hand was forced closer and closer to the black-rimmed mouth above the whirring, lethal blades.

That's when she heard Dawn's voice again,

deadly calm. "If you touch my stuff again, you fat brat, I'm not going to just jam your hand into the disposal, I'm going to jam your face."

Suddenly, Tillie fell to the linoleum. The garbage disposal clicked off as mysteriously as it had clicked on.

"D-Dawn?" Tillie stammered. "Is that you, Dawn?"

No one answered.

Tillie fisted off her tears and curled up on the kitchen floor, too afraid to move. Her big sister was obviously some kind of witch.

And that witch wanted her dead.

CHAPTER 4

Clark hung up his flannel shirt and pulled off his T-shirt. Then he slipped off his jeans and pulled on the raggedy, baggy pants that were part of his costume as Flunky Number Two. He felt fortunate that he was a flunky and not a Musketeer. They would be wearing tights.

Clark shuddered. *Not even for Lana would I appear in public in tights.*

"Clark?"

Clark turned to find Mike Karn looking at him. As in, star-of-the-play Mike Karn. Clark was a flunky, not to mention a lowly underclassman. Frankly, Clark was surprised that Mike, a senior, even knew his name.

"What's up?" Clark asked.

Mike fiddled with the oversized prosthetic Cyrano nose, which he hadn't yet glued over his own. "So, listen. I need someone to run lines with me."

"Meaning —?" Clark pointed at himself.

"Dawn said she'd do it, but she disappeared on me. And frankly, you're the only one in here. You mind?"

"No problem." Clark straddled a chair and reached for his script, even though the gesture was just for show. After reading the play a few times the night before, Clark found that he had it memorized. "Where do you want to start?"

Mike tapped his knuckles against the side of his head. "How about a memory microchip implanted in my brain? This part is a monster. Dawn's role is peanuts in comparison. I'm sure if she could have talked Gullet into casting a female Cyrano, she'd be — ouch!" Mike reached for his shin.

"Cramp?" Clark asked.

Mike rubbed his leg. "It felt like someone just kicked me. That hurts."

"You need ice?" Clark began to rise, but Mike waved him down.

"I'm okay. Page one hundred six. The balcony scene. Where Cyrano hides in the dark and pretends he's Christian because he's too afraid to tell Roxanne that he's in love with her."

It was Clark's favorite scene. He knew all too well how it felt to love a girl who was in love with someone else.

"I'll skip Roxanne's lines," Mike went on. "If I don't know a line, I'll call, 'Line,' and you give me the first couple of words, okay?"

Clark flipped open to the right page. "Okay."

With his eyes closed in concentration, Mike began to recite. "'Never until tonight have I spoken to you from my heart, fair Roxanne. Here in the dark, I feel free to speak the truth, without fear of being mocked. At last I say the words: I love you. . . .'" He hesitated and opened his eyes. "Line."

"'Only now do I know —'" Clark prompted.

"'Only now do I know the true meaning of love,'" Mike continued. "'I would give up . . .' Damn. Line."

"'I would give up my happiness to see you joyful,'" Clark read.

"Right, right," Mike frowned. "'When I look at you, I feel . . .'"

Clark finished the line for him. "'As if I could bring the stars down from the sky.'"

"I *know* that line!" Mike groaned in frustration. "Why can't I get this?"

Someone knocked on the dressing room door. Mike grabbed his script as Clark went to answer the knock. It was Clark's good friend Chloe Sullivan, notebook and pen in hand.

Chloe took in Clark's bare, muscular chest with appreciation. "No need to dress on my account, Clark."

"What are you doing here?" Clark asked.

Although Chloe barely came up to Clark's shoulder, she tried to peer around him into the dressing room. "Looking for Mike K — and there you are."

Chloe swerved around Clark and sat down next to Mike, who still had his face buried in his script. She waved her hand between his face and the pages. "Hel-lo? I'm Chloe Sullivan, editor of the *Torch*. You promised me an interview for the school paper. You were supposed to meet me yesterday. Remember?"

"I couldn't make it," Mike said tersely.

"Yeah, I gathered that. After I waited for an hour." Chloe opened her notebook to a list of questions. "So, Mike —"

"Yo, Barbara Walters? This is the *guys'* dressing room," Mike interrupted.

"Talented *and* observant," Chloe marveled. "Who could ask for more?"

Mike rubbed the bridge of his nose. "Look, Chloe, I'm not trying to blow you off. I just really have to work on these lines."

"Just a few questions, I promise," Chloe said. "Mr. Gullet has given my friend Pete permission to take photos during rehearsal, so you won't even have to smile for the camera."

"Mike, you might as well give in," Clark suggested. "She's relentless."

"You forgot to add 'in a charming sort of way,'" Chloe said sweetly. "So, Mike. You're playing Cyrano. Your real-life girlfriend is playing Roxanne. In the play, Roxanne loves another guy, Christian. What is that like for you?"

Mike shrugged. "It's acting."

"Got it." Chloe scribbled his answer in her

notebook. "Your role of Cyrano is much larger than her role of Roxanne. But you both want to be professional actors. Which one of you has more talent?"

Mike scowled. "That's a dumb question."

"Do you think she'll become more famous than you will?"

"What kind of an interview —"

"Sources close to Dawn report she has publicly stated that she believes she's more talented than you are. How do you feel about that?"

Mike stood up abruptly. "This interview is over."

Chloe stood, too. "But I'm just getting started —"

"Jeez, I don't have time for this crap now!"

Chloe put pen to paper. "May I quote you?"

"Come on, Chloe, cut him some slack," Clark murmured. "He's trying to learn his lines."

Chloe backed toward the door. "So I would be correct in reporting that only a few days before opening you don't know your —"

"Out!" Mike thundered.

"Bye." Chloe slipped out of the dressing room. Mike slammed the door after her. "Sorry, Clark. I know she's a friend of yours. I'm just stressing big-time."

"If you'd shown up at the interview you scheduled with her yesterday, she wouldn't have been in your face today," Clark pointed out.

Mike scratched his chin. "You think Dawn really said she's more talented than I am?"

Clark shrugged.

"She probably did. She told me my interpretation of Cyrano sucks."

"Not very supportive."

"No kidding. The chick psyched me out, got me thinking I can't do the part, you know?" Mike confided. "That's why I don't have the lines down. It's like she's got to constantly be the center of attention and she resents the fact that I have the lead. I'm telling you, she's whack." He put both hands on his head and stared up at the ceiling. "I have no idea why I'm saying this to you."

"I'm pretty good at keeping secrets," Clark assured him.

"Yeah?" Mike sat down and leaned toward Clark, dropping his voice confidentially. "When Dawn and I hooked up, it was wild. She'll do anything for attention. My friends were like, 'Your girl is so hot,' I was into it, right? So one day, out of nowhere, she tells me she's bored. Turns out, she goes through guys faster than a bean burrito. Once Dawn's been there and had that, she's on to the next."

Clark had no idea what to say. "I'm sorry to hear that. The two of you seemed really good together. You both want to act. And she's incredibly talented."

"Bull," Mike snorted. "As my Uncle Bubba in Texas would say, 'The girl is all hat, no cattle.'"

"But she's the best actress in the school," Clark protested.

"Yeah, just ask her," Mike sneered. "I'm telling you, the chick is plastic. Her personality. Her talent. Even her . . ." He cupped his hands in front of his chest and made a squeezing motion. "Last year Dawn was a 34-A. This year she's a 34-D. Do the math."

Clark was appalled at Mike's crudeness. "How

can you talk about her that way? I mean, it's none of my business. I know you guys have problems. But can't you work it out? You love her, right?"

"Love her? I don't even *like* her." Mike stood in front of the mirror and put on his Cyrano nose. "Once the play closes, she's history." He checked his watch. "We'd better get out there."

As soon as they left the dressing room, Mike's street clothes levitated. Then, they floated into the bathroom, where they took a swim in the urinal.

Dawn was P.O.'d, which seemed appropriate as she flushed the urinal. She'd thought being invisible in the guys' dressing room would be so much fun. The last thing she'd expected to hear was Mike dissing her to Clark Something-or-other. Well, Mike was going to pay. Big-time.

Livid as she was at Mike, she couldn't help but notice what a great bod this Clark guy had. Not only that, even though he said he didn't know her, he had defended her against the slings and arrows of that hemorrhoid, Mike.

Very impressive. Indeed.

ꕥ ꕥ ꕥ ꕥ

A half hour later, Lana, Clark, Chloe, and Pete sat with the cast and crew in the auditorium. A camera hung from Pete's neck. Onstage, Mike and Dawn were doing the balcony scene. Mr. Gullet stood a few feet away, watching them intently.

"I thought you told me this would only take an hour, Chloe," Pete groused, checking his watch.

Chloe shrugged. "Mr. Gullet said no photos until after this scene. It messes up their concentration or something."

"Yeah, well it messes up my life if I flunk math."

Chloe popped a stick of gum in her mouth. "If you spent half the time studying that you spend complaining, you'd be Stephen-flipping-Hawking."

"He's a physicist, Chloe," Clark whispered.

She gave him a dignified look. "I know that."

"Hang in there," Lana murmured to Pete. "They'll move on to another scene soon."

Pete looked up at Mike, who had just forgotten

his tenth line in the past ten minutes. "Not at the rate he's going." His eyes slid from Lana to Clark, then back to Lana. "So, where's Whitney, anyway?"

"Mr. Gullet asked him to pick up the new computerized lighting board," Lana replied. "It was delivered to the LuthorCorp factory."

"Oh." Peter eyed Clark significantly. "So that means *Whitney isn't here.*"

Lana looked perplexed. "I just said that."

Pete leaned over to Clark. "Ask her to get a cuppa with you, man," he hissed to Clark's ear. "While the competition is away, Clark can play."

"Can't," Clark whispered back. "We're not on break."

Pete folded his arms. "Your problem is you don't break enough rules."

"Uh-huh." Clark leaned forward, watching Mike onstage, struggling with the scene.

I don't like the guy, but I do feel for him, Clark thought, as Carrie, the stage manager, prompted him again.

"It might make it easier to work on the scene if you had bothered to learn the lines," Mr. Gullet said, loud enough for everyone in the theater to hear him.

Mike reddened. "I know them. Where was I?"

"'To say I love,'" Carrie called to him.

Mike nodded. "'To say I love you, such small words carry the weight of my entire . . .'" He groaned. "My entire what?"

"Soul," Clark muttered.

Onstage, Mike started anew. A moment later, he flubbed again. In the house, Clark quoted the correct line: "'I could happily die if just this once you'd gaze down upon me and declare your feelings match my own.'"

Pete glanced over at Clark. "What'd you do? Memorize the play?"

"Kinda," Clark admitted.

"How much of it?" Chloe asked.

"Uh . . . the whole thing."

Lana's eyebrows went up. "Very impressive, Clark."

Clark smiled at her compliment. "I'm sure it's tougher to remember lines when you're up there and the pressure is on."

An angry outburst from Mr. Gullet got their attention, as Mike stumbled over yet another line. "Mr. Karn, what is your difficulty?"

"His 'difficulty' is that he sucks," Dawn said hotly. "How can I be expected to stay in character under these circumstances?"

"Take a break, you two," Mr. Gullet said. "Mike, get your script. I want you to have it in hand for the rest of rehearsal. We open in two days. I know you know these lines."

Pete nudged Clark. "You know 'em better."

Mike slunk offstage. With an irritated hair toss, Dawn joined Missy and Julie in the auditorium aisle not far from Clark. He could hear everything they said.

"Can you believe him?" Dawn asked, flipping her hair again. "Like learning his dialogue is too much to ask."

"Welcome to amateur hour," Missy sympathized.

"You're so far beyond these little school plays, Dawnie," Julie agreed.

"Tell me about it." She rubbed her temples.

"That gave me a migraine. I've got stuff for it in my dressing room. I'll catch you guys later."

Dawn strode off, so Pete slunk down in his seat and closed his eyes. "I can't take photos if the stars are gone. Someone wake me when they start again."

Chloe elbowed him hard.

"Ow!" He rubbed the spot she'd poked. "What was that for?"

"A gentle reminder that you're here to work. Take some candids or something."

"Your poke is my command," Pete grumbled. "But at the rate this dude forgets his lines, we'll be here til the next millennium."

"Maybe you should do the role, Clark," Chloe mused. "You seem to know the lines. And at least I'd get a halfway decent interview with you."

Lana eyed Clark curiously. "How'd you memorize *Cyrano* so quickly?"

Clark shrugged. "It just sort of . . . happened." He watched as Mike came back onto the stage, script in hand. He mouthed the lines, desperately trying to commit them to memory.

One moment, Mike was still. The next—*wham!* As if he were smashed in the side by an invisible wrecking ball, he crumpled to his knees.

"What the . . . ?" Pete said, noticing. "That's weird."

"I better check to see if he's okay," Clark told his friends. He headed down the aisle toward the stage as Mike rose unsteadily, shaking his head to get the cobwebs out.

"Are you all right?" Clark asked, approaching the orchestra pit.

"Yeah," Mike replied. "I guess. I don't—"

Before Mike could complete his sentence, he grunted loudly and crashed off-balance into the pit. Instinctively, Clark dove and slid his hands under Mike's head just before it cracked into the concrete floor.

But Clark was too late to save Mike's leg. There was an audible *crack* as the actor's right fibula smashed into a folding chair, followed by an animal-like howl of pain that involved no acting at all.

CHAPTER 5

"Mike, honey, hang on. You're going to be okay." Dawn squeezed his hand as paramedics carefully loaded Mike onto a stretcher.

"I'll make sure he gets into the ambulance. Dawn, you stay here," Mr. Gullet instructed her. "Mike, I called your parents. They'll meet you at the hospital."

The theater was uncharacteristically quiet as Mr. Gullet followed the paramedics out to the ambulance. No one knew what to do or say.

Suddenly, Dawn whirled on the group. "Who saw what happened?" she demanded. She turned on little Jenni. "Did you see?"

Jennie shrugged helplessly. "He fell, I guess. It was during the break —"

"I *know* it was during the break, you imbecile," Dawn broke in, her tone scathing. "I was taking one, in the dressing room. That's why it's called *break.*"

Jenni's lower lip quivered. Lana went to stand by her. "I know you're upset, Dawn. But it's not Jenni's fault."

Tears pooled in Dawn's eyes. "You're right. Sorry, Jenni. I'm just so distraught. I don't care what Gullet said. I've got to go make sure Mike is okay." She ran from the theater.

Pete took this in. "Wow. She must really love the guy. Man, you never know, huh? One minute you have the lead in the play and a hot girlfriend, life is sweet. The next minute — *bam* — you're Humpty Dumpty."

Chloe peered into the orchestra pit. "Well, I'd say Humpty just earned freak of the week status. We're talking possible Wall of Weird material here."

The Wall of Weird was the giant collage Chloe had created in a room adjacent to the *Torch* office. It featured articles and photos about the bizarre, unexplained phenomena that often occurred in Smallville.

"Come on," Pete chided. "The guy was distracted, he was studying his script. He lost his balance and fell. Big bad deal. Nice save, Clark, by the way. You have the fastest reflexes in Kansas."

"I was closest to the aisle, that's all," Clark said.

Chloe tapped her pencil against her chin thoughtfully. "Unless Mike was suddenly overwhelmed by the desire to take a swan dive — which would be understandable considering that he's got like a zillion lines, he knew maybe three of them, and the play opens soon — he didn't just 'fall,'" she insisted. "Something pushed him."

Lana looked bemused. "I realize strange things have been known to happen around here, but in this case, Chloe, I have to say that you have a very vivid imagination."

"This is Smallville," Chloe reminded her. "In Smallville, you don't *need* an imagination."

"There's another problem here, anyway,'" Lana said. "Mike doesn't have an understudy."

Clark was surprised to hear this. "Why not?"

"They barely got enough guys to do this play in the first place," Lana explained. "No one wanted to memorize the role of Cyrano knowing he'd never get to go on."

"Yeah, well, you guys are looking at *never,*" Pete pointed out.

"This sucks," Mark Warsaw, a good friend of Mike's who played Christian, the guy Roxanne loved, chimed in from behind them. "We might as well put up a closing notice."

"We can't just . . . just cancel the play!" Carrie sputtered. "We've been working our butts off on this for months."

"Yeah, well, without Cyrano, you kind of can't put on *Cyrano,*" Mark said with disgust. "Of all the crappy luck."

As everyone argued about what they should do, Dawn and Mr. Gullet rejoined them. Dawn's eyes were red-rimmed from crying.

"Friends, Romans, Smallville thespians," an exhausted-looking Mr. Gullet intoned, which got their attention. "First of all, let me assure you that Mr. Karn apparently has nothing worse than a badly broken leg. We are, as you know, without an understudy. Therefore, I am open to even semibrilliant suggestions as to how we might salvage this production." He scanned the group. "Anyone? Anyone at all? Don't everyone hold back at once."

No one spoke.

"Maybe someone could go on script-in-hand," Carrie ventured halfheartedly. "And before anyone says anything, I know that idea blows. Cyrano can't duel with his eyes on a script."

"Hey, maybe you could play the part, Mr. Gullet," Jenni suggested.

"Please. He's old enough to be my grandfather!" Dawn exclaimed. "That crosses the 'ick' line, no offense."

"Yes, well, thank you for that ageist assessment, Miss Mills," Mr. Gullet said. "Not that I'm pining to be Cyrano to your Roxanne, I assure you. But unless someone a bit closer to your age knows the role, then I —"

"He does!" Pete blurted, pointing at Clark.

"Shh," Clark hissed.

Pete was insistent. "Hey, Mike's big break could be your big break."

"Thank you, Mr. Sensitive," Chloe muttered.

Pete turned to Mr. Gullet. "I'm telling you, Mr. Gullet, Clark Kent has this puppy down cold."

Mr. Gullet cocked his head at Pete. "And you would be?"

"Pete Ross, sir."

"And Pete Ross is not involved in this play, correct?"

"Taking photos for the *Torch*," Pete reminded the director. "But just ask Clark. He knows it."

The director looked at Clark. "Well, Mr. Kent?"

Clark felt like a deer caught in someone's headlights. *Where are Peter Pan's flying wires when I need them? I'd be out of here so fast —*

Suddenly he felt Lana's hand on his arm. "You do know the part, Clark," she said, her voice low. "I heard you."

"I'm no actor, Lana."

"You can say that again," said a familiar, cutting voice. Whitney.

I guess he's back from getting the lighting board. Great timing.

Lana regarded her boyfriend. "Do you know the part, Whitney?"

Whitney folded his arms defensively. "No. But like Kent said, he can't act."

That irked Clark. It was one thing for him to dis himself, and another thing to have to take it from Whitney. "What I meant was, I don't have any experience," Clark qualified. "Not that I can't do it."

"Do you know the role of Cyrano or don't you?" the director prompted.

Clark took a deep breath. "I do," he admitted.

"Might I hear the beginning of Cyrano's infamous monologue, after the young man insults the size of Cyrano's nose?"

Clark cleared his throat and began to recite. "'Your insults are lacking, young man. A nose such as mine deserves better. You could be witty: "Your nose is so large, you must drown when you drink!" Or: "Your nose is so heavy, it must hurt to think."'"

"See, he knows it!" Pete crowed.

"And I think he'll fit right into Mike's costumes," Carrie put in eagerly.

The director nodded, then slowly held out his hand for Clark to shake. "Well, well, Mr. Kent. Congratulations. It turns out you really are saving the day after all."

Does he mean what I think he means?

Clark panicked. "Wait! I mean, there must be another solution —"

"No other is needed," Mr. Gullet declared. He turned to the group. "Cast and crew, say hello to our new Cyrano de Bergerac, Mr. Clark Kent."

CHAPTER 6

"Run that by me again, Clark?" Martha Kent asked. Clark had rushed into the kitchen as she was making dinner, babbling something about the school play and "my big, fat mouth."

Clark plopped himself down at the kitchen table. "Just what I said. A guy at school fell and broke his leg during rehearsal."

Martha gave the spaghetti sauce a stir. "Is he okay?"

"I think I kept him from cracking his skull open," Clark allowed. "Don't worry. No one saw anything weird." He put his head in his hands. "What am I going to do? How did I get myself into this?"

"Into *what?*" She began to wash some lettuce for a salad.

"Mom, focus. Lana told me they needed replacements for some small parts, so I went to play practice to help out. Only now I have the lead. *Cyrano de Bergerac,* I'm Cyrano. And it opens in two days."

Martha turned off the water and regarded her son. "You're kidding."

"Do I look like I'm kidding?"

"But . . . I saw *Cyrano* in college. It's one of the most difficult parts ever written. You've never even been in a play before. This doesn't make any sense."

"That's exactly what I'm trying to tell you."

"Start from the beginning," she suggested. "And here." She handed her son a knife and a cutting board. "Use some of that excess energy to chop up the vegetables."

"It's all because of my stupid memory," Clark explained, as he superchopped the vegetables, his hand and the knife a blur. "I wasn't even trying to learn the whole play. It just *happened.* There has to be some way I can get out of this, Mom."

"It's not like you to just give up, Clark."

"Aha!" Clark's finger stabbed the air in his mother's direction. "I knew you'd say that. This is not 'giving up.' You can't give something up unless you tried to do it in the first place. Which I didn't."

Clark saw his mother draw in her cheeks. "Please don't hit me with the 'Clark, you're making excuses' face," he said. "This is not an excuse. This is a fact-based panic attack."

Martha smiled as she began wiping off the counter.

"You're happy about my misery?" Clark implored.

"Of course not, Clark." Martha turned to her son. "I was just remembering how I used to panic before school band concerts — I was tenth flute or something. But you. . . . I've never seen you in this state before. Just like any other kid."

"Swell."

"Mr. Gullet wouldn't have cast you if he didn't think you could do it," Martha pointed out.

"He did it because he didn't have any options." Clark swallowed hard, suddenly imagining himself frozen in place onstage before an audience of hundreds. "What if I ruin the play for everyone? What if —"

"Hey, you two," Jonathan Kent greeted them as he swung through the kitchen door. "Oil's changed in the tractor." He kissed his wife and then dipped a spoon into the bubbling spaghetti sauce on the stove.

"Jonathan," Martha reprimanded, but there was a smile on her face.

He slurped with gusto. "Terrific. Clark, it took me fifteen minutes to find the funnel for the oil. A place for everything and everything in its —"

"Place. Sorry." The oil-change funnel was the last thing on Clark's mind.

"Our son has news," Martha said. "Tell him, Clark."

Clark did. When he finished, his father looked bemused. "I didn't know you were interested in theater, son."

"I'm not," Clark blurted out, then realized how ridiculous it sounded. "I mean, I love this play. But I never even thought about . . . I have no idea what to —"

"Lana's on stage crew," Martha filled in.

"Ah," Jonathan said. He knew how his son felt about the girl next door. "Well, I'd say you should look at this as an opportunity."

"An opportunity to humiliate myself," Clark said, bemoaning what he saw as his probable fate.

"Look, I have a sense of what's really going on here, Clark," his dad said gently. "You can't use superpowers to be an actor, right? It's going to require you to be . . . human. Which means taking risks. Something that, when you think about it, you're not that used to doing. Not in a human way, anyway."

Clark felt his breath catch in his throat as he recognized the truth of what his dad had just said.

It's amazing how often Dad can put his finger on something that's bothering me, even when I'm not sure what it is.

"I guess that's it," Clark admitted.

His mom hugged him. "Personally, I think you can do anything you set your mind to, sweetie."

"Even this?"

"Even this," Martha said. "One thing I do know for sure, Clark. The only way you can fail is if you give up on yourself before you even try."

"I'll second that," Jonathan chimed in.

Clark sighed. In theory, he agreed with his parents. But neither of them would be up on that stage, ruining the play for everyone. Still, he was grateful for their support. "I suppose two out of three isn't so bad."

"Greetings," Chloe called, as she breezed in. She sniffed the air. "What smells so dee-lish?"

"Pull up another chair, Chloe," Mother said good-naturedly. "It's like you have some kind of mental telepathy. You always seem to know when it's spaghetti night around here."

"I have spies," Chloe said, wriggling her eyebrows. "Anyway, it's not my fault if you make the best spaghetti in the western world, Mrs. Kent."

"Flattery will get you everywhere. Could you grab the salad?"

Chloe brought the salad to the table and sat down. "So did Clark tell you he's about to become a star?"

Martha chuckled. "Not in exactly those words."

Chloe turned to Clark. "I figured if I did a quick yet remarkably insightful interview with you tonight — you know, the whole instant-star angle — I could still get it into the *Torch* that comes out the day of the show. This kind of thing is the stuff of legend."

"More like infamy," Clark muttered.

Chloe plucked a carrot from the salad bowl and nibbled on it. "Look at it this way, Clark. How many school activities are you really involved in? You went out for football for like three days but didn't get into a game. You wouldn't even give blood at the blood drive. Maybe it'll turn out that the theater is your big calling in life. You really do need to get an identity."

Clark shared a look with his parents.

If she only knew.

"Speaking of theater . . ." Chloe pulled an envelope from her backpack and handed it to Clark. "Photos. One-hour developing at the drugstore. They're Pete's. Meaning they're bad. From rehearsal this afternoon."

"I was there. I lived it. Do I have to live it again?" Clark asked.

"There is method to my madness," Chloe insisted. She leaned toward Clark, as he dutifully went through the shots. "Wait, stop there. There's Mike just before he did his swan dive. Okay, now look at the next one."

Clark did. Pete had snapped Mike's photo as he was tumbling into the orchestra pit. Chloe tapped a finger against the photo. "Well?"

"Well what?"

Chloe looked exasperated. "Well, doesn't it look like something is pushing him?"

Jonathan smiled as he set the glasses on the table. "Sleuthing again, Chloe?"

"Look closely at Mike's body," Chloe insisted. "He buckles at the knees, see? Like someone hit him in the back of the legs."

Clark gave her back the pictures. "No one is there, Chloe."

"No one that we can *see,*" Chloe clarified.

"Dinner," Martha called. She carried a heaping bowl of spaghetti to the table. Chloe slipped the photos into her purse as the Kents sat down.

"Just don't discount the possibility that something Wall of Weird–ish is going on here, Clark," Chloe added. "That's all I'm asking."

"The weirdest thing I can think of right now is that I'm supposed to play love scenes with Dawn Mills," Clark said, passing the spaghetti to Chloe. "It's like casting Natalie Portman as Roxanne and Tom Green as Cyrano."

As they ate, Clark's parents and Chloe kept up their pep talk, and Clark finally resigned himself to his fate. He'd just have to do the very best he could do and hope that it would be good enough.

When Chloe had arrived, she had left the screen door slightly ajar. She and the Kents were too busy eating to notice the door open, ever so slowly, another inch. Even if they had seen, they would have chalked it up to the wind that blew that night across the Kansas prairie.

They had no way of knowing that Dawn Mills stood near the refrigerator, invisibly watching them. Clark had just likened her to Natalie Portman. She smiled broadly, congratulating herself on her good taste; she had been right to sneak into Clark's house to see what she could learn about the guy. Under that boyish gee-whiz exterior, he was quite the hunk. And he had the good sense to appreciate her for the true talent that she was.

Fortunately, Clark thought ridiculous Chloe's little theory about Mike's accident *not* being an accident. Amazing that Chloe had been so accurate. Because Dawn knew she had aimed at the back of Mike's knees when she'd pushed him into the orchestra pit. If only he'd crashed right into the pit, instead of stumbling first.

As dinner continued, Dawn strolled closer to the table, taking in the way Chloe looked at Clark. It was patently obvious that the little twit had a crush on him. Dawn coolly assessed the competition. Chloe's hair was a mess, her body average, her face boring, and the alt clothes thing . . . so Ani DiFranco-last-century-Lilith-Fair-get-over-it-already. Meaning Chloe Sullivan was no comp at all.

Dawn smiled again, recalling her brilliant performance that afternoon, how she'd cried on cue over Mike's terrible tragedy. Now *that* was talent.

Well, Mike got exactly what he deserved. He was history. Dawn knew what she wanted now. She wanted Clark Kent.

And Dawn Mills always got what she wanted. Always.

Chapter 7

Dawn could hear the shower running in the bathroom as she padded invisibly around Clark's room. She imagined Clark dripping wet and in the buff. But, much as she would have liked to check it out, she had more important things to do. There would be plenty of time for that sort of sexy little romp when she and Clark were a couple.

And they *were* going to be a couple. Of that she was certain.

So, what did All-American Buff Boy read, anyway? She picked up a book. *Blue Highways*. She vaguely recalled seeing that on her family's bookshelf. What else? *Don Quixote*. She knew the musical version of that one. *Man of La Mancha*.

They'd almost done it last year at Smallville High and she would obviously have been cast as Dulcinea. *To Kill a Mockingbird.* She'd seen the black-and-white movie version on cable.

On a lower shelf she found an assortment of magazines: *Spin. Popular Science.* Something called the *Edge.* She flipped through it and found that it was a hip music rag. Duly noted.

She could still hear the water running, so she made her way over to Clark's music collection and pawed through the CD jewel boxes. Lots of Bob Marley reggae, alt stuff like Radiohead and Papas Fritas, retro bands like Santana and the Beatles, and everything from Dave Matthews to Barenaked Ladies — the guy's musical taste was all over the place. She opened his CD player. Marley's *Greatest Hits* was the last thing he'd been listening to. Dawn wrinkled her nose. Reggae was so boring.

She went to his closet. There were shirts half-on and half-off the hangers, a jumble of sneakers, jeans on the floor. Clark sure had a lot of sweaters, almost all of them blue or red. She held one to her nose. It smelled like him. Yummy.

The shower was still going. Dawn felt almost luxurious, strolling invisibly around Clark's room, exploring. She looked in all the places a guy would hide stuff from his parents — under his bed, the back of his closet, the bottom of his underwear drawer. It was kind of disappointing. No porn. No hidden drugs or alcohol. Not even a cigarette. The guy was a walking advertisement for clean living.

Dawn checked out Clark's desktop computer. It was on a flying-through-space screensaver. How cosmic. Idly, she touched one of the keys, and the monitor flashed to the start-up screen for Clark's Internet service provider. She froze. What if Clark came back and saw the screensaver was gone? He might know that someone had been in his room!

As if to underscore her fear, she heard the shower stop. Though she knew she was invisible, she still instinctively looked for a place to hide, hunkering down on the far side of Clark's bed. She peered over at the computer, praying for the screensaver to return.

He was coming. She could hear him humming

some reggae thing out of tune as he walked into his room, clad in a towel around his waist, drying his hair with a second towel.

Dawn looked past him toward the computer monitor, praying he wouldn't turn around. A nanosecond before he glanced at his computer screen, it flipped back to the screensaver. Dawn exhaled the breath she hadn't even realized she had been holding.

Clark froze. Had he just heard something? Was someone in his room? He felt as if something or someone beside himself was in there. He scanned the room with his X-ray vision: Into his closet, under his bed.

Nothing.

"Weird," he mumbled, chucking the wet towels into a laundry bag on the back of his door.

Dawn ogled him. Evidently, talented and sweet All-American Buff Boy had any number of strong suits.

As Clark pulled on his University of Kansas gym shorts, Dawn edged against the wall to be sure she wouldn't be in his way. After all, he might not be able to see her, but if he ran into her, he'd certainly be able to feel her. Besides, Clark was still a little wet. If water touched her, she'd become visible. That did not fit into her game plan at all.

She watched as Clark got into bed and turned out the lamp on his nightstand. Dawn waited, listening to his breathing. She wondered what he'd do if she crawled into bed with him, right that instant. It was almost too tempting to resist.

From Clark's breathing, she could tell that he'd fallen asleep. Slowly and carefully, she crept to his bed and gazed down at him. He was asleep on his back, one arm flung over his head.

"You're going to be mine, Clark Kent," she told herself silently.

The danger in what she was about to do sent shivers up her spine. She didn't care. Dawn leaned down and planted the softest of kisses on Clark's lips.

Then she fled into the night.

ꕥ ꕥ ꕥ ꕥ

School ended at noon the next day due to teacher conferences, which allowed the crew to put the finishing touches on the set before rehearsal. Clark went to the Beanery, hoping to find a quiet table where he could do some work on *Cyrano*. Mr. Gullet had met with him that morning and given him a script marked with a simplified blocking scheme.

"If you don't get it all, don't worry, Mr. Kent," the drama coach had said. "This is an emergency situation, and the cast will work around you. Just do your best at rehearsal this afternoon."

Clark knew that he could easily memorize the blocking. That wasn't what worried him.

"Stop," he said out loud, as if mere words could interrupt the loop of anxiety that had been plaguing him all day.

Concentrate. He flipped his script to the balcony scene.

"One love, one heart, let's get together and feel all right. . . ."

Behind him, some girl was singing softly. If it had been any other song, Clark could have managed to block it out. But this was Bob Marley's anthem, "One Love." He turned around. Dawn stood there, swaying to music coming from her headphones.

"Hey, Clark!" she said brightly, lowering the volume and pushing the headphones down to her neck. She noticed his script. "Going over the blocking?"

He nodded. "At least maybe I won't run into anyone onstage."

She slid into the chair across from him. "Not to worry," she assured him. "I'll help you every step of the way. Besides, the most important thing is for you to be Cyrano up there. Let the rest of the cast follow you. *You're* the star." She touched Clark's arm for emphasis.

Right, Clark thought, as Dawn's hand lingered on his forearm. *More like I came from a star.*

He jutted his chin toward her CD player. "You a Bob Marley fan?"

"The biggest," Dawn confessed. "I have all his CD's, and a bunch of bootlegs, too, that my cousin brought back for me from Jamaica. Why?"

"I love his music," Clark said. "Play it all the time. He was really a messenger of peace, you know?"

Dawn nodded vehemently. "Totally. There was a great article about him in the latest issue of the *Edge*. It's a pretty obscure magazine. I could lend it to you, if you —"

Clark was floored. "Wait a sec. How do you know the *Edge?*"

Dawn shrugged. "It's great. You can't get it around here, though."

"I know," Clark agreed, laughing. "My parents bring it back for me from Metropolis."

"Nice parents." She swung her backpack off her shoulder. "This thing weighs a ton." A heavy book fell out onto the table. Clark read the title. *Don Quixote*. Cervantes. It was just about his favorite novel of all time.

Dawn saw him looking at it. "I've read it like a dozen times, but every few months I take it out again. It's about —"

"I know what it's about. I *love* that novel."

"No kidding?" She leaned toward him, holding his gaze with her feline emerald eyes. "So,

Clark. It seems like we have more than acting in common."

"Yeah," Clark agreed. "It's kind of amazing, actually."

She ducked her head shyly to one side. "I hope you don't think this is too forward, but . . ." Dawn faltered, then laughed at herself. "Everyone thinks I'm so self-confident just because I'm an actress. But when you really like a guy. . . . I'm just going to come right out and tell you, Clark," Dawn went on. "From the moment I saw you I felt this . . . I don't know . . . connection with you."

"Must have been that hot flunky costume," Clark joked.

Dawn laughed. "Seriously." She reached across the table for his hand. "I think it must have been destiny that you're going to be Cyrano."

"What about Mike?"

Dawn looked blank for a moment. "Oh, him." She took her hand back and quickly slid a look of deep concern onto her face. "That was so terrible yesterday, wasn't it?"

Clark nodded. "I called the hospital this morning

to see how he's doing. His leg's broken in two places, but they're releasing him today. I'm sure you already knew that."

"Right," Dawn agreed, though she hadn't really checked on Mike and had no idea how he was doing. From her point of view, the butthole was lucky he was still *alive.* "It's a shame that it took a tragedy to bring us together, Clark," she said fervently, "but . . . well, it's not like we had anything to do with it."

"Bring us together . . . onstage?"

"Exactly," she purred. "I know you're nervous. It helps if you find something about your character that speaks to something that is true about you."

Clark looked blank.

"Take the balcony scene, for example. Have you ever been in love, Clark?"

"I'm . . . not sure."

"Then use your imagination. Close your eyes." She reached over the table again to squeeze his hand. "I can help you, really. But you have to close your eyes to concentrate."

"You're the pro." Feeling ridiculous, Clark closed his eyes.

"Okay. You're Cyrano. The greatest swordsman who ever lived. Brilliant with words. The only thing you lack is confidence in your physical appearance because of your huge nose. Can you picture that?"

"I'm working on it," Clark said.

"I'm Roxanne, the beautiful girl you love. Only you've never been brave enough to tell me that. Because I'm the kind of girl every guy wants. It's starting to bore me. What really gets to me is a guy who is great with words. So I fall for this hot guy, Christian, who writes me the most amazing, sexy letters. But what I don't know is that it was really you writing the letters for him. He's actually an IQ-free airhead. How would that make you feel?"

Clark thought about it a moment. "Terrible."

"Good," Dawn encouraged him. "Now, take the balcony scene, for example. You hide under my bedroom window. In the darkness you pretend to be Christian. You confess how much you really love me. Isn't that beautiful?"

"It's sad, actually." Clark opened his eyes.

"But, see, now you're putting feelings to

character, which is the start of acting," Dawn explained. "I want you to know, Clark, that I'm here for you. Day. Or night. In fact, after rehearsal tonight, maybe we can —"

"Clark?"

Lana was walking toward him, carrying a to-go coffee.

"Hey, Lana." As always, he tried to sound casual with her. He wasn't sure if he was succeeding.

"So, how's the Cyrano work going?" she asked.

Clark held up the script and shrugged. "I'm trying."

"I have faith in you, Clark. You're going to be terrific."

Dawn coldly eyed the girl sharing gooey grins with her soon-to-be-new boyfriend, Clark. This was no Chloe type. Clark was looking at this babe in a way she'd never seen him look at anyone.

Competition radar on high alert, Dawn tossed her blond mane off her shoulders. "And you would be —?" she asked imperiously.

"Oh, sorry," Clark said quickly. "I should

have. . . . Lana Lang, meet Dawn Mills. Dawn, Lana."

Dawn looked her over. Exotic and petite. Great-looking, if you were into her type. "Aren't you Whitney Fordman's girlfriend?" Dawn asked.

"Interesting thing to be known for," Lana mused aloud.

"Either you are or you aren't," Dawn said icily.

Instead of answering, Lana sipped her coffee, and then asked, "How's Mike? That was really awful yesterday."

"Right. Poor Mike," Dawn snapped. "Listen, we were just in the middle of rehearsal, Linda —"

"It's Lana," Lana corrected.

"Uh-huh. Aren't you selling programs or something for the play?"

"Stage crew."

"Then shouldn't you be in the theater right now, hammering away at those pesky last-minute details?"

"I came on a coffee run," Lana explained, looking over her shoulder toward the counter, where the waitress was filling two cardboard carriers with cups of coffee. She turned back to Clark. "I have a suggestion. I'd be happy to come over to the loft tonight and run lines with you."

"Great idea!" Clark exclaimed.

"Except that he'll be working on his lines with me," Dawn corrected. "You know. His costar. Though it was sweet of you to offer," she added hastily.

"Actually, I'd feel a lot more pressured with you, Dawn," Clark said.

"But —"

"I'll work with Lana tonight. Tomorrow you'll see how much I've improved," Clark continued. "That way I won't waste your time. Great idea, Lana."

"Fine," Dawn agreed, even though she was steaming. But it wouldn't serve her purpose to let on. After all, she had all the power here. She could use her invisibility to do whatever she wanted.

As for this Lana chick: Please. Okay, so she had a certain soulful-eyed, wounded bird thing going on. She reminded Dawn of a character she'd played in *The Glass Menagerie*, except that character had a limp and wasn't as pretty as Lana. Not that Lana was all that pretty, of course.

As Clark and Lana discussed rehearsal plans, Dawn's mind raced. No way was a dewy-eyed little nobody going to get Clark instead of her. No possible way. That thought made Dawn feel a whole lot better. Her mind cranked into overdrive, as she considered all the wonderfully hideous ways she could take down Lana Lang.

CHAPTER 8

Dawn gazed into Clark's eyes. "How do you feel?"

"Like midgets are playing roller hockey in my stomach," Clark replied.

She stood on her toes to kiss his cheek. "Don't worry, you're going to be wonderful."

They were at the theater, in full costume, waiting for rehearsal to begin. Mr. Gullet had told them there would be some scene work for Clark's benefit, and then a full run-through with lights and tech.

"Just remember the stuff we talked about," Dawn urged. "Imagine that you really are in love with me. That shouldn't be too hard."

"Right now it's hard to imagine anything except terror." Clark licked his lips. "My mouth is so dry. That's nerves, I guess, huh?"

Dawn nodded. "Why don't you get some water? There's still time."

"Good idea. Be right back." As Clark headed for the backstage drinking fountain, Dawn's two friends, Missy and Julie, sidled over. The three girls watched Clark as he bent over the fountain to drink.

"Poetry in motion," Dawn drawled appreciatively. "Don't you agree?"

"Absolutely," Julie agreed.

Dawn looked at Missy. "Well?" She asked, her voice sharp.

Missy hesitated. She was getting tired of sucking up all the time. But to disagree with Dawn could be dangerous. She was rich, gorgeous, and, in the social strata of Smallville High, very powerful. If Dawn didn't have to spend so much time on her acting, she would have been head cheerleader, easy. She gave the best parties, wore the hippest clothes, and took friends with her on family trips to Hawaii. She was also a predator who would toy with you one minute and, if she felt like it, devour you the next.

"He's cute," Missy agreed. "But, Dawn, aren't you in love with Mike?"

"Please," Dawn scoffed. "He's toast. Can you believe he thought he could act? What a joke."

Julie and Missy exchanged a look. Dawn was done with Mike Karn?

"He was never even in your league, Dawnie," Julie assured her. "What's up with you and this guy, Clark?"

"Nothing," Dawn replied. "*Yet,* that is." Dawn crooked her pinky finger and held it up. "But he'll be right here as soon as I want him."

"You're so bad!" Missy said, laughing.

Dawn laughed, too. "And I'm so good at it."

"Places in five," Carrie called, walking across the stage. "Balcony scene."

Dawn waved at her friends. "Buh-bye. That's my cue."

"Wait, Dawnie," Missy called. "We're still doing manicures after rehearsal, right?"

"Yeah." She splayed her hand, looked at her

nails, and frowned. "This French manicure is so boring. I'm going back to my usual, I don't care what Gullet says."

She headed up the steps and into the balcony just as Clark returned from the water fountain. She blew him a kiss from the balcony. He gave a halfhearted wave back, already feeling thirsty again. How was that possible?

Lana walked over to him. "You okay?"

"Does terrified qualify as okay?"

"Everyone knows you got thrown into this at the last minute," Lana reminded him. "Most guys wouldn't have stepped up to do the part, even if they did know the lines." Clark caught her glancing at Whitney, who was joshing around with Mark Warshaw behind a flat. "For what it's worth, Clark, I consider it quite heroic."

"Thanks. I think."

Lana smiled. "Well, I'd say break a leg, but after what happened to Mike, I'll just say good luck."

He nodded and crossed to his place onstage, underneath the balcony. Clark went over the scene in his mind. He was Cyrano. He was in love with Roxanne but afraid to tell her that he loved her. Hidden by the darkness, pretending to be Christian, he could confess —

"Ready when you are, Cyrano," Mr. Gullet called. He'd taken a seat in the front row of the house. With a start, Clark realized that Mr. Gullet was speaking to him. He nodded. It was all he could manage.

"We'll pick it up after Christian stumbles and Cyrano begins to speak for himself from the shadows," Mr. Gullet requested. "Roxanne, give Cyrano his cue."

Dawn closed her eyes a moment and then opened them fully in her Roxanne character. "'But Christian, why are your words so hesitant?'"

Clark gulped. The theater was deafeningly silent. And his mouth was so dry. He knew it was his line. He was sure of it. He knew the line. It was . . . it was . . .

"'Night has come,'" Carrie prompted from the wings.

Right. "Night has come." That was it.

"'Night has come,'" Clark began, so softly that he was pretty sure no one had heard him. He repeated the line. "'Night has come!'" Now he bellowed. Oops. Way too loud. After that, there was silence. Seconds ticked by.

"It's your line, Cyrano," Carrie called from the wings.

"Right!" Clark cleared his throat. "'It is a cloak that hides my words.'"

"'Surely you've no need to hide your words from me, Christian,'" Dawn replied. "'It is your words I so love. But I wish to see your face.'"

"'No,'" Clark said. "'I want to savor the moment, this rare occasion when sight is not between us. Our heads can speak —'"

"'Hearts,'" Carrie corrected. "The line is: 'Our *hearts* can speak.'"

"Right," Clark said. "I guess a head can't speak," he added nervously. No one laughed at his joke, so he continued, "'Our hearts can speak the truth when our selves are unseen.'"

"'Why unseen, Christian? You've no need to hide your heart from me.'"

"'Never until tonight have I spoken to you from my head—I mean, my heart,'" Clark stumbled. "'Here in the dark, I feel . . . I feel . . .'"

Frantically, Clark searched his mind. It was a total blank. A void. He had nothing. He heard other cast members mumbling in the wings. He was sure he knew what they were saying:

"The play is doomed. Kent is ruining everything."

Then, an image of Lana popped into his mind. Watching him, in his moment of failure. Feeling terrible. And disappointed.

And Whitney. Gloating.

"'I feel free to speak the truth,'" Mr. Gullet prompted from out in the house, where he sat, taking notes. "I was under the impression you knew these lines, Mr. Kent."

Clark looked out into the house. "I do, sir. I'm just nervous, I guess."

"All right, then, Clark. That's understandable. But please concentrate."

Clark nodded. He squeezed his eyes shut. Maybe if he just read the words he saw in his mind's eye, he'd be okay. He inhaled deeply, and then began to recite. "'I feel free to speak the truth without fear of being mocked at last I say the words I love you only now do I know the meaning of true love.'"

He risked a peek out at Mr. Gullet.

"That was three sentences, Mr. Kent," the director pointed out. "A period at the end of a sentence implies that you stop. Then, you say the next sentence. That's how it works."

Clark nodded. "Right. I know. Sorry. It's just that —"

"And what was that little peek at me earlier? You never break character and look out into the house. You are Cyrano. There *is* no house."

"Uh . . ."

"There is an invisible fourth wall in the theater, Mr. Kent. One you cannot see through. The audience is beyond that. Meaning you don't see me. Meaning don't ever make eye contact with anyone in the audience again. Ever. Clear?"

"Yes, sir."

The director's voice grew kinder. "I know you're nervous, Clark. And we're all feeling a little on edge. It would help if you could deliver the lines with some passion. Or are you unfamiliar with the emotion?"

Clark reddened. "I can do it better, sir. Really."

"Wonderful. I'd love to see it."

They began again. Clark bungled his way through the scene. He wasn't just bad. He was awful. The worst. A disaster. Finally, the scene was over. Clark stood on the stage, as alone as he'd ever felt.

I wish there were a trapdoor underneath me. Because right now I would gladly fall through it.

"Ten-minute break," Mr. Gullet announced wearily.

Clark trudged offstage. No one spoke to him. He went into the house and dropped into a seat at the back of the auditorium.

"Hi." Dawn sat down next to him, her face a mask of compassion.

"I know I messed that up," he told her. "I'm really sorry, Dawn."

She touched his biceps. "I know how nervous you are," she said soothingly. "It's okay. You'll be better during the run-through. And by tomorrow, you'll be fantastic."

"I wish I could believe that."

Her emerald eyes captured his. "You need to trust me, Clark. I know that if I work with you, you can do this. I really think I should come over to your house later so that we can work together."

"But, Lana —"

"Little Lana-Banana hammers nails into the set," Dawn interrupted. She put her index finger to Clark's lips. "But I'm your Roxanne. Which one of us is going to help you more?"

"Lana, I think," Clark replied. "She's as much of an amateur at this as I am. Working with you is . . . kind of intimidating."

"Whatever you think is best, Clark." She leaned over and whispered in his ear. "There'll be plenty of time for us later."

Clark watched her walk away. *What did she mean by that?*

"Interesting girl," a familiar voice said. Clark craned around to see Lex leaning casually against one of the auditorium's rear doors. "There's something reminiscent of *Fatal Attraction* about her. Ever see it?"

Clark shook his head.

"Bad date rental," Lex said, strolling over to Clark. "So, this is rehearsal."

"What are you doing here?" Clark asked.

Lex slid into the seat next to Clark's. "I told you. I'm the play's benefactor. I thought I'd check out the progress of this little endeavor."

Clark groaned. "Please don't tell me you just saw that."

"All right. I won't tell you."

Clark slunk down in his chair. "Fine. Great. I'm sure you're sorry you ever agreed to invest a penny in this."

"My motivation was more community relations than Broadway hit, Clark."

"Tell me the truth, Lex. I can take it. How bad was I?"

"Monumentally."

"Thanks."

Lex leaned toward Clark. "There is hope, however."

"I doubt it."

"Seriously. I think I can help you."

Clark's gaze was dubious. "You can act?"

Lex smiled thinly. "An art I've perfected for most of my life. Haven't you heard that all the world's a stage?"

"Right now I'd happily zip off to some other world where acting doesn't exist," Clark confessed.

"Well, sorry to break it to you, my friend, but unless you have information that the rest of humanity lacks, this is the only world we've got. Therefore I suggest we both make the most of it. I feel quite certain you can do this, Clark."

"Based on?"

"Call it the intuition of a rather brilliant friend if you like," Lex offered. "Stop over to my place when you're done here. I'll take it from there." He stood. "Look at it this way, Clark. You've saved my ass a number of times. And now, I get to return the favor."

ꕥ ꕥ ꕥ ꕥ

Pretty Nails had opened in a storefront on Smallville's Main Street a month earlier. It was owned and operated by Vietnamese immigrants who charged less than half of what the longtime Smallville beauty shops charged for a manicure, and it was doing a brisk business. You could also get your legs waxed or get a tan in one of the tanning beds in the back rooms. And they always played loud rock and roll.

Dawn and her friends had become regulars, stopping in for weekly manicures. Ignoring warnings about tanning and skin cancer, the three girls had also taken to using the tanning beds in pursuit of a year-round glow. An hour after *Cyrano* rehearsal ended, the three girls walked into the salon together.

"Basically, Clark sucked at the run-through," Missy said, as she held the door open for her friends. "You would have been a lot better off with Mike."

"Wrong," Dawn said blithely. "Clark Kent is pure untapped potential."

"Are you sure?" Julie asked tentatively.

"Who knows more about acting, you or me?" Dawn snapped.

"You, Dawnie," Julie assured her. "Maybe he'll get better."

"He will." Dawn idly perused the large assortment of nail polishes that Tran, the woman who ran Pretty Nails, had put out on the front counter.

"Dawn!" Tran called. She sat at her work station, finishing up on a customer. "I got in a new shipment of Blue Moon! From Metropolis!" She held up the small bottle of silvery-blue nail polish.

Dawn flashed Tran an "OK" sign. She'd first read about Blue Moon in *Vogue*. Then Tran had pointed out that it complemented her skin tones. Dawn had been wearing it ever since. It was her signature nail polish.

"Dawn, Gullet said you can't wear blue nail polish during the play, remember?" Missy reminded her.

"What's he going to do, fire me?" Dawn asked. "Besides, he'll be too busy with all the last-minute details to even notice I have it on."

Tran had finished with her customer, so Dawn

sat down at her station. While Tran went to work on her nails, Missy and Julie had their own manicures done. Then they'd all use the tanning beds.

"So, did you hear from Juilliard yet?" Missy asked Dawn.

Dawn had done a regional audition in Metropolis for the prestigious New York acting school. It rankled her that she hadn't gotten an acceptance letter yet. "If I had, don't you think I would have mentioned it?" she asked icily.

"Everyone knows you'll get in," Julie assured her.

Missy nodded. "You are going to be a major star."

Dawn smiled at her friends. "You two can run my fan club."

"What color?" The nail tech asked Missy.

"None." Missy's eyes slid over to Dawn. "You may have the nerve to defy Gullet, Dawn. But you're the star."

"No color for me, either," Julie told her tech.

Dawn laughed. "You two are such wusses!"

Julie and Missy finished their manicures quickly. After that, another tech led them to the tanning rooms. "Room One's ready for you girls," she said, opening the door to the tanning room. "Your friend gets Room Two when she's ready."

Just as Tran finished Dawn's manicure, Tran's cell phone rang. She answered it and began talking in rapid Vietnamese. Putting her hand over the phone, she told Dawn, "Go dry your nails under the special light. I'll be right there."

Dawn read a supermarket tabloid while her nails dried. When she finished, Tran was still on the phone, arguing loudly.

"Tran?" She called impatiently.

Tran covered the phone again. "My boyfriend got a speeding ticket in *my* car. The police are saying the registration is no good. But —"

"Right, whatever. I'm kind of in a hurry."

Tran took a key from her drawer and handed it to Dawn. "You're a good customer. Let yourself in Room Two, okay?"

"Thanks, Tran." With the key dangling from her finger, Dawn went back to the tanning rooms and unlocked Room Two, careful not to nick her silvery-blue nails. She was undressing to get onto the tanning bed when the strangest thought crept into her mind: *I wonder what Missy and Julie talk about when I'm not there.*

She smiled. There was an easy way to find out.

She took the glowing green rock from her purse and rubbed it over her feet and calves. The rock worked its magic. Soon she was entirely invisible, right down to her newly polished nails. She peered at herself in the mirror on the wall of the tanning room. She wasn't there.

"Too cool," Dawn told her invisible reflection. "Time to have a little fun."

Dawn padded down the hall and slipped into Room One. Missy and Julie were on their tanning beds, eyes covered by protective goggles. They were yelling to each other over the piped-in rock music.

"See the look on her face when I told her how talented she is?" Julie asked. "Oh, the best was when I told her she was better looking than Gwyneth!"

"And more talented," Missy hooted. "She totally believed you!"

They both cracked up.

Dawn was stunned. They couldn't be talking about her. It had to be someone else. Yes. That had to be it.

"Dawn is so totally played," Missy went on. "She's done, like, every hetero guy in drama club. She's totally pathetic!"

"You bee-otch!" Julie catcalled with glee.

"I'm so sick of sucking up to her," Missy said. "She's all like, 'Look at me, I'm so cute, I'm so talented, me, me, me.' Well, if Dawn didn't have cool toys and a hot car, no one would hang with her."

Dawn froze. Those . . . those witches. *Traitors.* Pretending to be her best friends and talking smack about her behind her back. They were as bad as that sphincter, Mike. No, they were worse. Everyone knew that your best girlfriends were supposed to always be there for you. They deserved to suffer for being such two-faced liars. And not just suffer a little, either.

Dawn edged over to Missy's tanning bed. The "Ultraviolet Intensity" knob was set at 3, on a scale that went to 10. Next to the "Ultraviolet Intensity" knob was a timer. A brass sign was above both dials:

CAUTION! *DO NOT* SET INTENSITY ABOVE 5 FOR LONGER THAN FIVE MINUTES. LIFE-THREATENING BURNS COULD RESULT. PRETTY NAILS IS NOT RESPONSIBLE FOR MONITORING USE OF TANNING BEDS.

Dawn cranked the intensity knob to 10. She swung the timer from fifteen minutes back around to sixty minutes. Then she slipped the shoelace out of Missy's sneaker, looped it around the handle of the tanning bed, and knotted it. No way could Missy open that tanning bed now, no matter how hard she tried. She did the same thing to Julie's tanning bed.

"Buh-bye, girls!" Dawn sang out. "Don't stay in too long, now!"

"Did you say something, Julie?" Missy called out.

"Nope!" Julie yelled back.

Dawn managed to stifle her laughter. But before she slipped out, she reached for the volume control on their room sound system and cranked it up as loud as it would go. Better safe than sorry. She wanted to make absolutely certain that no one would hear her so-called friends scream in agony as they fried.

CHAPTER 9

Clark pressed the doorbell at the Luthor mansion. A pretty young woman clad in jeans and a T-shirt with the Beatles on it opened the door.

"Hi," she said. "I mean, good evening."

"Hi, I'm Clark Kent —"

"Yeah, right, he's expecting you." She ushered Clark into the front hallway. "Mr. Luthor is downstairs in the armory. This way." They started down the hall together.

Though Clark usually hung out with Lex in his library, he'd been in the armory a few times. It was a cavernous hall where various instruments of war from ages past — some of them worth a fortune — were displayed. There were swords, crossbows, muskets, antique pistols, maces, and even suits of armor. Lionel Luthor collected them and used the armory room as a place for storage.

"Excuse me, I didn't catch your name," Clark said.

"I didn't throw it," the girl joked. "It's Tatiana. I have a horticulture company. Mr. Luthor hired me to take care of the houseplants. The butler has the day off, and the maid's in the loo, so she asked me to answer the door if you showed up before she got back. This formality thing is kind of new to me."

"I don't think Lex would mind."

"Yeah, well, I don't get to call him 'Lex.'"

Tatiana and Clark descended the stirs and stepped into the armory. Lex was waiting for him. "Welcome back to the lair of *guerre.*"

"French for 'war,'" Tatiana translated. "Not that it isn't fairly obvious."

"I see you lucked into a lovely escort, Clark," Lex noted. "The maid must be indisposed again."

Tatiana nodded. "Well, orchids await me. Unless there's anything else?"

"There is, actually." Lex wiped at a spot on his

sword's handle. "Have I mentioned that one of the qualities I like most about you is that you are honest?"

"You mean blunt," she corrected. "That's what everyone says."

"Exactly." Lex smiled pleasantly. "So, tell me, blunt Tatiana. If someone who had never met me asked you to describe me physically in one word, what would that one word be?"

She hesitated. "This isn't exactly in my job description."

"Humor me," Lex coaxed. "I'm eccentric."

Tatiana shrugged. "Bald. Sorry, but you asked."

"Yes, I did. Thanks. You can go."

Shaking her head over Lex's oddness, she left.

"Don't you find honesty refreshing, Clark?" Lex asked.

"As in, I honestly stink at Cyrano and this was your way of preparing me to face the truth?" Clark ventured.

"Yes," Lex agreed. "And no." He crossed to a rack of swords of different lengths mounted on the wall. "What shall it be, Clark? Sabers or foils?" With great deliberation he chose a sword with an ornate, filigreed handle and handed it to Clark. "Here. A foil worthy of Cyrano himself."

Clark hefted the sword and swung it. The lightweight blade curved back and forth with a whooshing sound. "The stage swords don't really have points on them," Clark said. "Which is a good thing, since I've never really fenced before."

Even with nubs covering the sword points I barely moved the sword around at rehearsal because I was afraid of hurting someone. Mr. Gullet tried to show me a few things, but I still looked like a total dork.

"How did it go after I left?" Lex queried.

"Would it be possible to be any worse than when you saw me?"

Lex grimaced. "That bad, huh? Assume a dueling position."

Feeling foolish, Clark did it.

"Needs work," Lex commented. "Video could be a big help to you, you know. Then you can see your mistakes."

"Imagining them is bad enough, thanks."

"I'll give you one of my video cameras before you leave. You can practice at home."

"It's a little late in the game for that, isn't it?"

Clark asked glumly. "After this — whatever *this* is — I'm meeting Lana to work on lines. Then there's another dress rehearsal tomorrow afternoon — called especially for the guy who is ruining the play, namely me. And then . . . well, that's it. My name goes down in the annals of Smallville theater infamy."

"There's a first time for everything Clark. Don't let the foil's light weight fool you. It can be quite lethal. Think: control. You begin like so." Lex took a fencing stance, left leg forward, the sword in his right hand extended upward behind him.

"There's the attack. . . ." Lex thrust his sword toward Clark. "The lunge, which is a strong push with the back foot that accelerates you toward your opponent — easy to explain, difficult to do." Lex lunged at Clark, who stepped backward. "The parry — that's your basic defense move, back and forth. And, of course, the hit, meaning you nick one of your opponent's target areas." Lex flicked the end of his sword near Clark's chest. "At which point you say, *'Touché.'*"

"All I'm doing is stage combat, Lex. You know. Fake."

Lex ignored him. "Dueling is essentially a genteel form of psychological warfare. And physics. To every action there is an equal and opposite reaction." He leapt at Clark, thrusting his sword forward. Clark automatically stepped backward.

Lex grinned. "Case in point."

Clark was bewildered. "You asked me to come over so that you could teach me to fence? What does that have to do with acting?"

"You are playing Cyrano de Bergerac, the greatest swordsman who never lived."

"What difference is it going to make how I swing around a fake sword?"

"This isn't about you, Clark," Lex said. "It's about a fellow named Cyrano."

Clark held the sword out to Lex. "You might as well take this. I appreciate that you wanted to help me, but I don't think learning to fence is my problem."

Lex indicated that Clark should keep the sword but put his own back in its sheath. "Clark, if you had to describe Cyrano to someone who didn't know him, in one word — no, give it two — two words, what would they be?"

Clark sighed. Clearly, Lex didn't intend to give up. "Large nose. Is there a point here, Lex?"

Lex smiled. "I told you about my first trip to Smallville, didn't I? I remember it so vividly. Like it happened yesterday." He strode over to a window and peered out, as if looking into the past. "My father and I arrived in his private helicopter. I was petrified. He hated me for that, of course. He hated pretty much everything about me. My fear. My asthma. My bright-red hair."

Clark's stomach did a loop-the-loop. He already knew this story too well. He carried the guilt inside of him all the time. Why was Lex reminding him?

"My father was getting some papers signed, so I got bored and wandered away," Lex continued, still gazing out the window. "It was a perfect autumn day. I snuck into a cornfield. The stalks were so thick they looked like trees. I remember feeling so happy, because I was nowhere near my father."

He turned back to Clark. "And then, Clark, I experienced the only thing that ever terrified me more than he had. That meteorite, rocketing to the earth behind me . . . exploding in a concussion of force and fire. When it was over, I lay in that cornfield. I couldn't speak, couldn't move. And I was completely and totally bald, for evermore. I was nine years old."

Clark barely nodded, not making eye contact.

I wish I could just tell him the truth. How I fell to earth with those meteors that day. I wish I could just say: "I'm responsible for what happened to you that horrible day, Lex. To everyone. It's my fault."

"Needless to say, permanent baldness became a defining feature of my life," Lex continued. "Much like having the world's most outsized nose. Which is why I've always related to Cyrano. He's brilliant, witty, talented, and yet he has this insecurity, based on that which defines him physically, above all else. I wonder, Clark. What defines you above all else?"

Clark forced himself to sound casual. "I'm an ordinary guy, really."

"We both know that's a lie." Slowly, Lex walked toward Clark. "You're as extraordinary as Cyrano, but in ways that don't meet the eye."

Clark laughed nervously. "I don't know what you're talking about."

Lex was only inches from Clark. "I will learn your secrets, Clark. It's just a matter of time. But back to me." He grinned and touched the top of his own bald pate. "I learned at an early age to beat others to the punch about this, as does Cyrano with his outsized nose. Early in the play, the viscount insults Cyrano's nose and Cyrano fights a duel with him, all the while spontaneously inventing clever rhyming insults the viscount *could* have used, if that viscount had any brains or creativity. It's utterly disarming. Cyrano wins the duel, both physically and psychologically. As you will, tomorrow night."

"Nice insight, Lex, but it's not going to make me into an actor."

Lex unsheathed his sword and assumed a dueling stance. "Your sword, Clark."

"Really, Lex, this is —"

"En garde." Lex declared, assuming his stance again. He lunged at Clark, who instinctively lifted his sword to defend himself, causing a zing of crossed blades.

"Come on, Lex —"

"You speak of my baldness with such banality, such utter lack of brains or wit?" Lex improvised, as he began a riposte attack. Clark instinctively parried. Lex kept coming, leaving Clark no choice but to duel with him.

"There are a hundred ways one might speak of my baldness," Lex went on, crossing swords with Clark again and again. "That is, if one were clever. The witty approach: But, sir, you look the same, from front or from behind. Your dermis is so bare that I can see what's on your mind!

"The comparative approach: Your head looks like a bowling ball, perhaps a giant Q-tip. Or wait, I know, a round, white board, let's slap on little Post-its!"

Lex thrust forward more aggressively now, steel clashing against steel. Clark parried, blocking Lex's attack and countering with one of his own, forcing Lex to back away.

Lex battled back. They crisscrossed the armory floor.

"One could say: Luthor gets brainwashed every time he takes a shower," Lex continued, his words punctuated by a Morse code of clashing steel. "Or: The man's head could be a sun dial upon which we read the hour."

"Very clever," Clark managed.

"I haven't finished," Lex said, blocking one of Clark's thrusts and adding one of his own. "Have I mentioned that in fencing a touch means a kill? Or would you rather play for blood?"

"Uh, touch is fine," Clark replied.

Lex nodded and pressed the attack again. "I conclude with the insult approach, beloved by those of limited brainpower, the darling of the dull, the litmus of the limited, to wit: 'Lex, have you three hairs upon your head? Or even less, perchance? So when you seek a barber, he must tell you: "Drop your pants!"'"

In a flash, Lex thrust his sword toward Clark's chest. Suddenly, Clark moved his body and sword so swiftly that the next thing Lex knew, his jugular vein was directly under the tip of Clark's sword.

"Clever, Lex," Clark said. "Really. *Touché*."

"Thanks." Lex eyed the point of Clark's blade.

"You're a natural at this. I'm glad we didn't decide to draw blood."

Clark moved his sword from his friend's neck, and Lex straightened up. "I still don't see the point."

Lex grabbed one of the monogrammed hand towels draped over a suit of armor and tossed another one to Clark. "Well, for one thing, you just proved that you could duel very convincingly."

"The only thing I'm convinced of is that you missed your calling. Maybe you should give up this business stuff and become a playwright."

Lex laughed, wiped his neck, and then slung the towel around it. He retrieved two blue water bottles from a refrigerator recessed into the wall behind a wooden panel. "I've got these refrigerators everywhere. One of my little idiosyncrasies." He handed Clark one of the bottles. "Here's the thing, Clark. You know Cyrano's weakness. I've told you mine. Yours may be hidden. But it's there. Imagine it being so exposed that the entire world, including the girl you love, knows that secret . . . whatever it is."

Images flew into Clark's mind, unbidden. Men from the government, taking him away from his parents at gunpoint. A *Daily Planet* headline: *Smallville Alien Confirms Extraterrestrial Life.* Himself, behind bars, caged like an animal in a zoo. . . .

Clark shuddered.

"Ah, I see I've hit a nerve," Lex observed, putting his foil back on the rack. "If you learn only one thing, Clark, let it be this: Acting is about baring your soul under the protective cloak of someone else's life. And that, my friend, is the end of my little lesson."

"Well, it was interesting, I'll give you that much," Clark said. He handed Lex his sword.

"Keep it," Lex insisted. "For luck. Legend has it that some swords have magical powers. Not that I believe in magic. Or in luck, for that matter. But, at the risk of drifting into the mawkish, Clark Kent" — he clinked his water bottle to Clark's — "I do believe in you."

Chapter 10

An hour later, Clark was up in his loft setting up Lex's video camera.

Not that I think it'll do any good. But at this point I'll try anything.

When he'd gotten home from Lex's, he'd nuked some leftover pizza while his parents quizzed him about the play rehearsal. He didn't have the heart to tell them how truly awful he'd been, but Martha and Jonathan could sense that it hadn't gone very well. They assured him it didn't matter if he wasn't a great actor. The important thing was, he was following through on his commitment. That was what made them proud of him.

They're so excited about coming to see me in the play.

No matter what they say, I know seeing me wreck everything is going to be a major disappointment.

So much for the video camera. It was ready. And Clark was as ready as he was going to get. He checked his watch. Lana was late. Who could blame her? He took a long gulp of water from the sports bottle he'd brought up to the loft. Who knew nerves could make a guy so thirsty?

Outside, he heard a horse whinny, followed by Lana's soothing voice. In spite of his worries, he smiled. His mom called it his doofus smile — the one that appeared on his face only when Lana was around. Well, he could take the teasing. He's seen the same doofus smile on his father's face sometimes, when his dad looked at his mom.

"I thought maybe you blew me off," he said, when she came into view up the rough-hewn wooden stairs leading to the loft.

"No chance. Sorry if I'm late. One of Nell's friends left us her horse to board while she's in Metropolis on business. I rode her over."

"No problem," Clark assured her.

"Her name is Yvonnette. Sounds cute, I know,

but her disposition isn't likely to get her voted Most Popular Mare in the Stable." She noticed the video camera pointing at them. "What's up with that? Going *Dawson's* on us, Clark?"

"Lex lent it to me. He said I should video our rehearsal. He thinks it'll help me. Which I would appreciate, if I wasn't pretty sure I'm beyond help."

"Lex is giving you advice on *Cyrano?*"

"I was at the Luthor mansion this afternoon," Clark admitted. "Working on the dueling scene with him."

"I see." Lana went behind the camera and looked at Clark through the viewfinder. "I'm feeling kind of guilty, Clark. I'm the one who got you into this."

Clark drifted over to the telescope that was by the window. Earlier, he'd had it focused on the Crab Nebula. There were so many stars out there, so far away. It glittered, beckoning to him. He wished he and Lana could leap toward the heavens and just keep going until —

"You can't run away from your fears, Clark,"

Lana said softly. "Wherever you go, there they are."

Freaky. It was as if Lana had read his mind. He turned to her. Her face was still partially hidden behind the video camera. "When did you get so smart?" he asked.

She lifted the camera, still running, off its tripod. "Actually, my aunt told me that. I have a feeling it's one of those wise little truisms that's easier to tell someone else than to follow yourself. You're very photogenic, Clark."

He shuffled his feet self-consciously. "I wish you'd turned it off until we start the scene."

"Why?"

"I feel like a bug under a microscope, that's why."

"Sorry." Lana lowered the camera, a pensive look on her face. "I was just thinking . . . how I always feel like people are looking at me. You know: 'There's that poor girl whose parents were killed in the meteor shower.' But just now, looking at you from behind the camera . . . it felt nice to be the observer instead of the observed."

Clark understood in more ways than she could ever know.

On some level, I'm always hiding. In the back of my mind, I always know that, above all else, I can't let anyone know the truth about me.

It's such a lonely way to live.

"Clark? You okay?"

He forced a smile. "Sure."

"What scene do you want to work on?"

Clark thought for a second, looking around the barn. "The loft is kind of like a balcony. Maybe if I go down there, you can stay up here and we'll do the balcony scene."

"Fine."

"Great." He took the camera from her, returned it to the tripod, and then repositioned it so that it would record him when he stood down below. What had he been thinking? The balcony scene was the big romantic moment of the play. Why had he ever thought it would be easier to rehearse a love scene with Lana than with Dawn?

The very fact that I don't care about Dawn took the pressure off. Whereas saying this stuff to Lana. . . .

As he turned away from the camera, his hand smacked the water bottle. It went flying, water shooting everywhere.

"Sorry." Clark said, red-faced. "Did I get you?" He could see that one sleeve of her denim jacket was wet.

"Don't worry about it," she assured him. "I don't melt."

"Right! Okay. So, I'll just go down there, I guess. Did you bring a script, or do you want mine?"

She bit her lower lip. "Actually, I kind of . . . know this scene."

He was surprised. "You mean I'm not the only one who does that?"

Lana looked embarrassed. "I guess between reading it and rereading it and being at all the rehearsals, I just kind of . . . learned it without really trying to."

He was standing so close to her. How was it possible for a girl to be so beautiful? What words could possibly express how he saw her, how he felt when he was near her?

Acting is about baring your soul under the protective cloak of someone else's life.

In that moment, with every part of himself that he knew, and parts of himself he hadn't yet figured out, Clark understood what Lex had told him. Cyrano's words came to his lips. "'When I look at you, I feel as if I can bring the stars down from the sky,'" Clark murmured.

His eyes held hers. There was nothing, and everything, between them. Clark could lift a truck with one hand. He could walk through fire untouched by the flames. But now he felt a kind of power different from any he'd ever known.

Finally, Lana spoke Roxanne's line. "'Your words glitter like stars,'" she replied. "'But are they true?'"

Clark turned, taking the stairs two at a time until he stood below, in the shadows, looking up at Lana. The moonlight danced in her hair. He called up to her.

"'Here in the dark, I feel free to speak the truth, Roxanne, without fear of being mocked.'"

"'Mocked for what?'"

"'Feelings. Honesty. The night is a cloak that hides my words.'"

"'You've no need to hide from me, Christian. It is your words I love.'"

"'Then let me speak, before I lose my courage,'" Clark said. The truth, Cyrano's and his own, came to his lips. "I love you. Only now do I know the meaning of true love. It means I would give up my happiness for the sake of yours, even without your knowledge —'"

From outside the barn, Yvonnette whinnied loudly, stomping her hooves, bringing Clark back to reality. It took him a moment to focus.

Oh, God. I just confessed to Lana that I love her. But they were Cyrano's lines. She doesn't know. I hope.

Outside, the horse whinnied again. Clark cleared his throat. "Want me to check on the horse, Lana?"

"I'm sure she's okay," Lana called down. "For a big girl, she certainly spooks easily. Sorry, I know she broke your concentration."

"It's okay." Clark scratched his cheek. "I thought that went . . . better."

"Better?" Lana echoed. Laughing, she ran down the steps and threw her arms around Clark. "You were *wonderful!*"

Clark was afraid to believe it. "I — really?"

"Really."

"It was the strangest thing. Something Lex told me suddenly clicked in my brain."

"Well, it was amazing," Lana insisted. "Almost as if you meant every word you were saying."

Because I did mean it.

In Clark's mind, those five words hung like a cartoon bubble over his head. He had no right even to think that. Lana loved another guy. Just like Roxanne loved Christian and not Cyrano. Better to keep it light. Talk about the play.

Clark smacked his thigh. "Well, all I can say is, hot damn, I don't suck!" With a whoop he lifted her in the air. They were both laughing breathlessly when he put her down, his arms still around her. He wanted to kiss her more than he'd ever wanted anything in his life. His face inched toward hers. She lifted her lips to his.

Outside, Yvonnette neighed anew. They broke apart, suddenly self-conscious.

"Something's up with that horse," Lana said, frowning. "She doesn't sound right."

They went outside to find the horse exactly where Lana had left her, tied loosely to the old-fashioned hitching post outside the barn. Yvonnette calmed as soon as she saw Lana.

"What's up, girl?" Lana asked, petting the horse's silky, dark neck.

Clark looked around. "I wonder what made her nervous."

"Maybe she stepped on something sharp," Lana said, still patting the horse. "You don't have the greatest of dispositions, do you, Yvonnette? Or do you just miss your human?" She glanced down at the luminous hands on her watch. "Wow, I had no idea it was so late. I should get going."

"Yeah, sure. Listen, thank you." Clark chuckled. "Yeah, that sounds completely inadequate. Really, though —"

"You're welcome," Lana interrupted. "But I always knew you could do it."

Clark felt lighter, hopeful. "I'm actually starting to believe it myself. I think I'll go back in and practice some more."

"Don't forget to sleep, Clark," Lana said playfully. "After all, you're only human."

Clark bit back his smile. "I'll try to keep that in mind. 'Night."

Chapter 11

Lana watched Clark return to the barn. He was such an enigma to her. She'd known him almost her whole life but sometimes felt as if she didn't know him at all. For example, he'd do something amazing, like saving Whitney's life. But afterward he didn't want any accolades. Well, tomorrow night, when Clark took his curtain call and everyone was applauding, he wouldn't be able to hide from the recognition he deserved.

She couldn't get over how much he'd improved since that afternoon's rehearsal, when he'd been on autopilot. But now, with her, he'd been . . . transcendent. So Lana couldn't help wondering: Had Clark improved because it was her playing Roxanne, instead of Dawn? In some way, had he meant the words he'd said? Or was that just wishful thinking, because in some way she meant them, too?

Somehow, Clark saw her differently than anyone else had ever seen her. And the Lana Lang she saw reflected in those startling eyes of his was the Lana Lang she wanted to be.

The horse nuzzled Lana's neck. "I know, Yvonnette. I have a boyfriend who loves me, and his name isn't Clark Kent. Enough dreaming. Time to go."

As Lana untied the reins from the hitching post, Yvonnette whinnied and stomped uneasily. "Hey, girl. It's okay. We're going home now," Lana assured her. But the horse whinnied again, twisting her head around, seemingly looking for something. This was strange. Lana peered into the night, trying to follow the horse's gaze. She saw nothing unusual.

"There's no one here but us," Lana reassured the animal. "You're okay, girl." She lifted one foot into a stirrup and swung the other over Yvonnette's back. But before she could slide into the other stirrup, the horse bellowed and reared up on her hind legs. "Whoa!" Lana shouted, as she grabbed the reins tightly. "Whoa, girl!"

The horse snorted and stomped the dirt, but Lana finally gentled her. "You're more temperamental than Dawn Mills," she told Yvonnette, then clucked her tongue and gave a gentle tug on the reins. "Let's go."

But Yvonnette refused to budge. "You and I need to come to an agreement," Lana told the horse, her irritation rising. "This is an interspecies partnership, and this is how it works: I give the signal, and you —"

Suddenly, the horse flailed wildly, rearing and bucking. It was all Lana could do to hang on.

Dawn stood near the barn. Watching Lana's struggle filled her with malicious glee. Her invisible right foot throbbed a bit, but hey, if you kick a big horse in the flanks a few times, your foot is bound to hurt.

Now all Dawn had to do was stop Clark from coming to the rescue. She knew he would; he was that kind of a guy. She hurriedly closed the barn doors, then jammed a two-by-four she'd found in the hay through the doors' handles. No way was Clark opening that from inside. By the time he found another way out, Lana would be thrown from the horse and trampled to a bloody pulp under Yvonnette's lethal hooves.

"Help!" Lana screamed, desperately trying to stay on Yvonette's back. "Clark, help!"

Lana! Clark ran to the loft window and saw the out-of-control horse trying to pitch Lana. He super-sped downstairs, tore across the barn floor, pushed the closed doors. . . . They hardly budged. He pushed harder. Still stuck.

How can this be? There's no lock on the barn door!

There was no time to ruminate. Clark took a step back and then rammed the double doors with his right shoulder. They shattered. Stifling a scream, Dawn hit the ground, as a half-dozen razor-sharp wooden torpedoes narrowly missed her invisible head.

"I can't stop her. Clark, help!" Lana yelled. With a ferocious buck, Yvonnette sent Lana flying. Clark dove fifty feet to slide his body between Yvonnette's hooves and Lana's back. An angry hoof smashed down on his neck, but he barely felt it. He wrapped his arms around Lana and rolled them a safe distance from the stampeding horse.

They were under a tree. Clark could feel Lana shaking in his arms, her heart pounding against his. He pulled away so that he could see her face. It was matted with dirt. "You okay?" he asked softly.

She nodded, then gently moved out of his embrace. She sat up and leaned against the tree.

Clark sat up, too. "What happened, Lana?"

"I don't know. It was crazy! Like . . . like someone was hitting that horse. God, Clark, if it wasn't for you . . ." Her voice trailed off.

He knew what she meant. If not for him, she could easily be dead.

She brushed some hair off her face. "How did you do that?"

"I just kind of, you know, slid."

"You *slid?*" She looked incredulous.

He nodded lamely.

"Well, all I can say is: Thank you. You saved Whitney's life once. Now I guess you've saved mine, too."

Whitney.

The last thing Clark wanted to think about right now was Whitney.

"Stay here, catch your breath," Clark told Lana. "I'll get the horse."

Yvonnette had galloped far into the field; then she'd turned around and trotted back toward them. She seemed much calmer now. Clark approached the animal, speaking softly. She let him take her reins and followed him to the hitching post, where he tied her up again.

Clark stroked the horse's sweaty neck. Something was bothering her. *Horses don't go crazy for no reason,* he thought. He eyed the woodpile that used to be the barn double doors. *And barn doors don't magically lock when they don't have locks on them.*

"You're staring at the barn like you're trying to see through it," Lana observed, as she walked over to him. "You sure *you're* okay?"

"I'm fine. Lana, did you notice anything weird when you came outside?"

She shook her head. "Yvonnette was acting strangely, though. Why?"

"I don't know," Clark said pensively. "But maybe there was a reason the horse got spooked, Lana, even if we didn't see it."

"Meaning?"

Clark turned to her. "Meaning, I have a feeling that what just happened to you might not have been an accident at all."

CHAPTER 12

Dawn brought her hand to Clark's cheek and tenderly spoke Roxanne's final lines. "'How could I have been blind for so long? It was you who loved me all along, Cyrano.'"

"'Yes, always,'" Clark replied. "'And I will love you until the day I die.'"

And that's all Rostand wrote, folks. I got through the special dress rehearsal. And I'm pretty sure I did not suck!

Offstage, a techie slowly lowered the curtain as Clark continued to gaze into Dawn's eyes. Clark and Dawn had been instructed to hold the final tableau until the curtain was completely down. But suddenly, Dawn's arms snaked around Clark's neck, and she brought her lips to his in a passionate kiss. Clark couldn't move without breaking character. He was stuck.

As soon as the velvet curtain made contact with the stage floor, Clark extricated himself from Dawn's embrace. Heartfelt applause exploded through the theater. The entire cast and crew was cheering, whistling, calling Clark's name.

As he pried the latex Cyrano nose from his face, guys ran to him and clapped him on the back; girls hugged him. "Swear to God, Kent, I didn't think you had a rat's ass of a chance to pull this off," Mark Warshaw admitted, as he heartily shook Clark's hand. "But you really came through."

Even Whitney offered up a grudging, "Good job, Kent."

"Magnificient work, Mr. Kent!" Mr. Gullet called from the wings.

Magnificent? From Mr. Gullet?

That's when it hit Clark: *I did it without any superpowers. I was the same as any other guy on this one, and I did it.*

"Hey, what about me?" Dawn asked the director, pouting prettily.

"Excellent!" Mr. Gullet pronounced. "I am a happy director."

Dawn rubbed up against Clark and sexily lowered her voice. "We were so hot together, Clark. I must have inspired you."

But Clark wasn't even looking at her. His eyes were glued to Lana, who headed over to them. Dawn's face went red with fury. If she had succeeded the night before, Lana wouldn't be striding *anywhere*.

"Congratulations, you two," Lana said graciously. "You were terrific. And I bet you'll be even better tonight in front of an audience."

Dawn hooked her arm through Clark's. "I guess I've finally found my match. Speaking of matches, shouldn't you be running off to find Whitney right about now?"

Lana didn't flinch. "I'd think that a girl whose two best friends landed in the hospital's burn unit yesterday wouldn't have any energy left to think about me."

"I'm desperately concerned about Missy and Julie," Dawn insisted, tugging Clark closer. "But as a professional, I have to put my personal concerns aside when I'm onstage."

Gently but firmly, Clark unhooked himself. He had no feelings for Dawn beyond admiring her talent; he was not into having her hang all over him. As he stood there between Dawn and Lana, their differences were starkly apparent. Lana had that which Dawn could only fake onstage: soul.

As Dawn tightened her grip on his arm again, something about her began to gnaw at the edges of Clark's consciousness.

"Well, excuse me," Lana began, "I have to —"

"Wait. Lana, where are you going to be later?" Clark asked. "I need to talk to you. It's important."

"I'm sure whatever it is can wait," Dawn said, an edge to her voice.

Lana ignored her. "You can call me later, Clark. I'll be home."

As Lana headed off, Chloe and Pete made a beeline for Clark. Chloe gave him a massive bear hug. "I have just witnessed the transformation of Clark Kent," she announced. "You were amazing."

Clark grinned. "Thanks."

"For real, Clark," Pete agreed. "I didn't know you had it in you."

"Unlike you two," Dawn said, "I *always* knew he could do it. Clark is a very passionate guy. *Very.*"

Chloe took this in. "Down, girl. Clark isn't on your to-do list, 'kay?"

Pete snorted back a laugh. Dawn glared at Chloe, but Chloe's attention was on Clark. "Seriously. I think you've finally found your career path. You could end up a movie star, or on a TV show, or —"

"Everyone is released," Carrie announced. "Mr. Gullet is one hap-hap-happy director, so he's saving notes until an hour before curtain tonight. Be on time." She looked at Pete. "Mr. Gullet said you can take those pictures backstage, if you still want 'em. Just follow me."

"He wants 'em," Chloe answered for Pete.

"Thank you, Madam Dictator — I mean Editor," Pete said. He slunk off with Carrie.

"So, Clark . . . do we have plans for this afternoon?" Dawn asked coquettishly. "You get so tense, but I know just how to relax you. Come to my place. My parents are taking my sister to dinner early. We'll have total privacy."

"I'm kind of busy now, Dawn," he said pointedly. "With Chloe."

Chloe pointed at herself. "That would be me."

Dawn's eyes darkened. "Fine. No problem. I'll see you tonight." She stormed offstage, pushing angrily past a couple of people who blocked her way.

"Okay, that chick is a serious head case," Chloe pronounced.

"You may be more right than you know," Clark muttered. "Let me get out of this costume and then we'll go to the *Torch* office. There's something I want to show you."

Chloe shrugged. "Sure. But don't you want to hear about Julie and Missy?"

"Of course I do. I'll be back in five minutes." Clark hurried to the guys' dressing room and was happy to find it empty, so he super-sped out of his costume and into his street clothes. Then he grabbed his backpack and zipped back to Chloe.

"Wow, quick-change artist," Chloe commented,

as they headed for the newspaper office. "You were gone, like, sixty seconds."

Clark brushed it off. "Oh, you know, guys are faster than girls. So, you were going to tell me about Missy and Julie?"

"Right. I went to the med center, like you suggested. The good news is that they're going to be okay. But we're talking serious shake and bake," Chloe reported. "Both girls have second-degree burns everywhere. And I do mean *everywhere*. Feel free to use that vivid Kent imagination. And get this, Clark," Chloe continued, as they pushed into the *Torch* office. "Julie told me someone tied their tanning beds shut. The police are treating Pretty Nails as a crime scene. I mean, it's pretty clear that it was deliberate."

Clark tapped one finger against his chin thoughtfully. "In some deeply sick way, this is all starting to make sense. Remember what you said about Mike's injury being Wall of Weird material?"

Chloe sat on the edge of the nearest desk. "Yeah, so?"

"Well, I'm starting to think that you're right. Is there a VCR around here?"

Chloe cocked her head toward the Wall of Weird room. "Back there. Why?"

"Come on." Clark led the way to the back room. He took a videotape from his backpack.

"What exactly are we watching?" Chloe asked.

"A tape from last night," Clark said. "Of me and Lana."

Chloe's eyes went hurt, but she covered quickly. "Back up, big guy. More than I need to know."

"We were *rehearsing,*" Clark clarified.

"Right." Chloe smoothed her tattered dignity. "I knew that. So why do I want to watch your rehearsal tape?"

"We. I haven't seen it yet, either. Our VCR is on the fritz." Clark relayed exactly what had happened the night before; how spooked Lana's horse had been when Lana had tried to mount it. It had been as if Yvonnette could sense something they couldn't.

"Yes!" Chloe cried happily. "It's the return of the Smallville ghost."

"Chloe, there never *was* a Smallville ghost."

"As far as you *know,*" Chloe said. Her eyes lit up. "Okay, maybe this is . . . the Phantom of the Auditorium. Who has it in for Lana. You're telling me you've got this ghost on tape? Can you tape a ghost?"

"The answer to both those questions is: I don't know, but we're about to find out." Clark slid the tape into the VCR and pushed a few buttons. The tape flicked on with Clark in the loft, pacing nervously before Lana had arrived.

"Reasonably cute guy," Chloe quipped. "Introduce me."

A moment later, they were watching Clark and Lana talking. The image wavered as Lana aimed the camera at Clark.

Chloe rolled her eyes. "This makes late-night C-SPAN seem exciting."

"The problem is, I don't know what I'm looking for. Let's fast-forward it."

"Oh, that'll make what you don't know that you're looking for so much easier to find," Chloe joked.

Clark couldn't very well tell Chloe that he'd be

able to see details of the tape even if it was on fast-forward. But it would save them both a lot of time. Chloe pressed the fast-forward button. Images on the TV monitor sped by.

"Stop," Clark commanded. He thought he'd just seen . . . something. "Back it up."

Chloe rewound the tape until Clark told her to stop. It was the moment when Clark had accidentally sent the sports bottle flying. "Nice touch, Clark," Chloe said, when she started the tape again. "Adam Sandler does Cyrano."

"Go back," Clark instructed, staring hard at the screen. "Now forward in slo-mo. Hold it there."

Chloe pressed the pause button. "What?"

Clark stared hard at the monitor. "Look."

"I *am* looking." All Chloe saw was Clark's frozen image, looking embarrassed at having just spilled water all over Lana. "Um, Clark? What exactly am I supposed to be looking for?"

"This." Clark grabbed a pencil from the desk and touched the graphite tip to the screen. "Right *there.*"

Chloe squinted at the screen. To the left of

Clark, maybe a foot off the ground, was something so bizarre that it was difficult to take it in, even for Chloe. "Umm . . . it looks like . . . a human finger," Chloe ventured. "Floating in space."

"That's exactly what it is," Clark said.

Chloe paled. "A dismembered finger? Isn't that a little too *Blue Velvet?*"

"It's Dawn," Clark pronounced, still staring at the screen. "I think she's responsible for all of these attacks. Somehow, she's found a way to make herself invisible." He pointed to the screen. "Except for that finger."

Chloe shook her head. "Yeah. That's a little whacked out, even for me. And you made this mental leap how, exactly?"

He pointed to the screen again. "See the silvery-blue nail polish on that fingernail? That's the color Dawn always wears. She's wearing it right now, in fact. Which means . . ." Clark jumped up. "Come on."

Chloe followed him out of the *Torch* office. "Where are we going?"

"To find Dawn," Clark replied, as they raced

back to the auditorium. "We have to stop her, Chloe. Before it's too late."

ꕥꕥꕥꕥ

Clark and Chloe disappeared down the hall. Outside the *Torch* office, in the seemingly deserted hallway, came the eerie sound of disembodied laughter.

Finally, Dawn caught her breath. They were all so stupid. Wasn't there anyone at all who was truly worthy of her, who wasn't a hypocrite or a liar?

At first she'd been livid. How dare Clark choose that silly little alt twit over her? It had been an easy matter to stay out of sight and follow them to the *Torch* office and then detour to the girls' bathroom to make herself invisible. When she returned, she found they'd left the *Torch* door wide open, so she just pranced into the Wall of Weird room and found them watching the VCR.

She hadn't realized that her finger had gotten

wet the night before when Clark went klutzoid under the spell of that insipid Lana Lang. It irked Dawn all over again that she hadn't succeeded in engineering Lana's demise the night before.

So, Clark's plan now was to track her down. Dawn figured he'd check backstage first. After that, he'd probably come to her house. She laughed again. She didn't live far from school. She'd be home before Clark arrived. So what if he knew the truth? *He didn't know that she knew he knew.* That gave her every advantage. He was coming over? Fine. Dawn would be waiting for him. Soon it would just be her and Clark. Forever.

CHAPTER 13

The knocker on the front door of the Mills' palatial home was shaped like a golden angel. Clark banged it impatiently. "Come on, come on," he muttered under his breath.

Finally, the door opened. A young girl with freckles and a ponytail stood there, holding a magnifying glass and a fist-sized quartz stone. "Hi," Clark said. "I'm Clark Kent, I'm in the play with your sister."

"Oh, yeah, I heard about you. I'm Tillie. Her sister. Have you ever seen quartz magnified? It's got cool colors." She offered him the quartz and magnifying glass.

"Thanks, but I really need to speak with Dawn," Clark said. "Is she here?"

"Yeah. She's upstairs in her room. Did you know my sister is a witch?"

"Dawn?"

Tillie nodded, then her eyes lit up. "Hey, what if it turns out she's actually the devil's spawn? That'd be *sweet!*"

A car pulled into the circular driveway in front of the house and honked impatiently. Tillie rolled her eyes. "My parents. We're going to dinner before we come see your play." She leaned close to Clark and spoke conspiratorially, her eyes solemn. "Last chance. I'd leave now if I were you."

"I'll risk it," Clark said.

Tillie shrugged. "Your funeral." She gave an eardrum-shattering yell over her shoulder. "Dawn! Cyrano's here!" She turned back to Clark. "Up those stairs. Don't worry. I'll tell my parents who you are."

"Thanks."

An even more impatient honk summoned Tillie. "Okay, okay, I'm *coming!*" she yelled. "Jeez, don't get a wild hair up your butt." She gestured Clark inside, then skipped out to the car.

Clark looked around. There was a grand staircase that led to the second floor. Clark headed upstairs, planning as he went.

Chloe's off making sure that Lana is okay. It'll just be Dawn and me. I have to convince her to get help before she hurts anyone else.

He reached the upstairs landing. "Dawn?" he called.

"Clark?"

"Where are you?"

"My bedroom. Down the hall!"

"Which door?"

This time Dawn didn't answer.

The first room had an open door. He looked inside. Tillie's room, obviously. He could tell from the boy-band posters and the endless shelves of rocks and minerals.

He opened the next door to what looked to be a guest bedroom. There was one more door past that. On it was a framed mock *Daily Planet* with the headline: "Dawn Mills Wins Oscar!"

Clark knocked. "Dawn?"

She didn't answer, so Clark opened the door

and looked around. The walls featured posters of all the plays in which Dawn had starred. There was a vanity table covered in a jumble of cosmetics and bottles. The window was open; delicate lace drapes fluttered in the slight breeze. Some of Dawn's clothes were piled on her canopy bed, as if she'd tried on and discarded various outfits. But no Dawn.

Unless she's invisible. How could I possibly tell she's here unless she speaks? My X-ray vision won't help. None of my superpowers will.

"Dawn, can you hear me?" He felt silly, speaking into thin air, but continued anyway. "I know what's going on, Dawn. We need to talk."

"Clark?"

Clark whirled. The voice had come from outside. He went to the open window and peered out. There were beautiful gardens, and a huge kidney-shaped swimming pool twinkling in the late afternoon sun.

The thought hit him like a thunderbolt.

What if it was the water I spilled last night that made her finger visible? If she's invisible now, and I can get her into that swimming pool, maybe it will make her visible again.

"I'm coming down, Dawn," Clark called, scanning the backyard. He didn't see her, but he knew she was down there. Somewhere.

"Great," she called back flirtatiously. "I'll be waiting."

He super-sped downstairs and into the backyard.

"Clark," Dawn whispered huskily. "I knew you'd come."

He was standing near the deep end of the pool. Dawn's voice had come from the direction of the pool house, near the shallow end. If he could just get a fix on her. . . . "Listen, Dawn, I know you can make yourself invisible."

"I was right about you," Dawn said. "I knew you were smarter than all the others. You can't imagine how powerful this is, Clark, to be invisible whenever and wherever you want to be. Oh, by the way, did I mention that I'm completely naked? Of course, I guess you'd have to do a touch test to confirm that."

Whoa.

Clark tried to banish the mental image and concentrate on the problem at hand. It sounded as though she had moved closer. He weighed the idea of jumping in the pool and causing a super-splash. If he caught her off guard, it could drench her. But the idea seemed risky — if she didn't get wet, she'd run away and he'd lose his chance to reason with her.

"Why don't you make yourself visible, so we can sit down and talk?" Clark suggested.

"Okay," Dawn agreed amiably. "But like I said, I'm naked. So I think it would only be fair if you took off all your clothes first. As a good faith gesture. Deal?"

"Uh . . ." Clark quickly X-rayed the pool house and saw bathing suits hanging on wooden pegs. "How about if we put on bathing suits?"

"Silly boy," she purred. "Why would we want to do that?" Now her voice was coming from near the diving board again. It was maddening how she kept moving. He had to keep her talking.

"How do you do it, Dawn? Make yourself invisible?"

"Magic," Dawn said softly. "A magic girl like

me deserves a magic man like you. Don't you think?"

"What I think is that you hurt some people. Mike. Missy and Julie —"

"What about how they hurt me? Everyone in that play is a liar. They're all talking about me. Do you think I don't *know?*" Her melodious voice rose to a screech. "They pretend to be my friends, then lie about me behind my back —"

"They were wrong," Clark allowed. "But violence isn't the answer."

"'Violence isn't the answer,'" Dawn mimicked Clark, her voice low. Then she laughed maliciously. "My darling Clark, Mike and Missy and Julie are basically human garbage. Trash must be disposed with."

"You don't mean that, Dawn."

"'You don't mean that, Dawn,'" she mimicked again. "Clark, Clark, Clark. You're not only talented, you're sweet and sincere and earnest. And you have a great ass. What girl could ask for more?"

"I'm your friend," Clark said firmly, "but there's nothing else between us."

"That's so sweet," Dawn trilled. "Don't you know that little Miss-Doe-Eyes-Ooh-I'm-So-Sensitive Lana Lang is not even in your league? I should have offed her when I had the chance."

Hearing Dawn say that so flippantly — she was somewhere near the lawn furniture, it sounded like — turned Clark's stomach. "You need help, Dawn."

"No, Clark. The only thing I need is you. At the end of rehearsal today, when I kissed you, I could tell that you felt the same way."

"Dawn —"

"Don't fight it, Clark."

Now she seemed to be near the cedar picnic table a few feet from the pool house. Clark hadn't noticed the washcloth and glass of water on the table until the cloth's edge dipped into the glass, then floated into midair.

"I'm the one you really want." Dawn's voice was a seductive whisper. The washcloth moved sideways, very slowly. Clark watched, astonished, as Dawn's collarbones became visible. They hung in the air like small, flesh-colored bird wings.

"Don't you get it, Clark?" Dawn continued.

"I'm a great actress. I can be every girl you ever dreamed of. Listen."

The next voice Clark heard was a perfect imitation of Lana's. "'You can call me later, Clark. I'll be home.'"

The washcloth streaked left to right, a few inches underneath the collarbones, revealing the underside of Dawn's breasts.

"'Down, girl. Clark is not on your to-do list, 'kay?'" Dawn chirped in perfect Chloe inflection. It was the most amazing thing Clark had ever heard. Or beheld.

"I never doubted your talent, Dawn," he said. "I just want to help —"

Suddenly, Clark saw the ribbons of flesh that Dawn had just revealed begin to fade. It was like a photograph developing in reverse. He was confused. "Did you just make yourself disappear again?"

"No!" Dawn sounded frantic. "What's happening to me? *What the hell is happening?"*

Clark edged toward her voice. "Dawn, stay still. I can help you."

"No!" She sounded on the edge of hysteria.

"Stay calm, Dawn." He reached out to where she'd been. "Take my hand. I'll wait for you. We'll go inside. You can get dressed and then we'll figure this out together. Okay? Dawn?"

He waited for the longest time, hand outstretched, hoping to feel Dawn's fingers in his. But he felt nothing.

ஐ ஐ ஐ ஐ

Dawn dashed inside the house and up to the bathroom. How could she have gone invisible again without using the green stone? She jammed on the faucets and shoved her arms underneath them. The water splashed over her. It had no effect. She dropped to her knees, hyperventilating with fright. The play started in three hours. She had to reverse the invisibility. *Had* to! She ran into the shower and jerked on the water. She could see it bouncing off her body. But there was no body to see. Oh, God, she couldn't reverse it anymore. What if she could never reverse it again? She'd be invisible and alone, forever. She might as well not exist.

It was the most terrifying thing she could think of.

And then, suddenly, it came clear to her, the destiny that was the love story of Dawn and Clark. Everything that had happened, all the humiliations she'd suffered, had been leading to this moment.

Clark was the only one who knew the truth about her. If she shared her invisibility with him, they'd be together as they were meant to be. They belonged together. They were eternal soul mates.

She scrambled back to her room and looked outside. There was Clark, still by the pool. She rushed to her closet and grabbed a floppy-brimmed hat, which she smashed onto her invisible head. Then she slipped into an oversized robe and went back to the window, pulling the hat down low over her nonexistent face. Clark was still there. Why, it was as if he were Cyrano, and she was Roxanne, up in her balcony. It was Kismet.

She leaned out the window slightly. "Cyrano?"

He looked up. "Dawn?"

"'Why hide in the dark when I long to see your face?'" she quoted from the play.

"Stay there, Dawn. Please. Don't move. We'll go to the med center. Everything will be okay."

"My Cyrano," she murmured.

Clark super-sped up to Dawn's room. But when he got there, the hat he'd seen in the window was on the bed, along with a robe. "I know you're scared, Dawn," Clark called out. "Please, let me help you."

"You care about me," Dawn whispered dreamily. The voice came from near her overflowing vanity table. "I know you do."

"Yes."

"I knew it," she exulted. "Poor Clark. You're worried that we can't be together now. But I have the power. I can make you invisible, too. Think of it."

"Dawn, no —"

"You can't imagine how wonderful it is. We'll be able to go anywhere, do anything. Our love will be stronger than windows or doors or —"

"Dawn, I don't love you." Clark's words hung in the air. "But I do care about you. And I will stand by you. We'll go to the police, and you can tell them —"

"I offer you everything, the greatest power in the universe, and you say you don't love me?" Dawn shrieked, as tears spilled onto her cheeks. But Clark couldn't see them. No one could. "Then why don't you *go to hell!*"

Suddenly, a large stone on the vanity table levitated and flew at Clark. He grabbed it — it felt like he was grabbing agony itself. The rock fell from his hand to the floor, shattering there.

Instantly, Clark felt sick to his stomach, so weak that he could no longer stand. He dropped to his knees. One of the rock chunks was directly in front of him. It glowed green.

Meteorite.

"Help me," Clark gasped, understanding his terrible predicament. "Please."

Dawn had no idea what was happening to Clark. Nor did she care. "To think I believed in you!" Dawn cried, fisting away her invisible tears. "You're just as bad as the rest of them. Everyone in that play deserves to die."

"No!" Clark tried to rise. His legs collapsed under him. "Dawn," he panted. "Please."

"Go ahead and beg," Dawn sneered, heading for the door. He was crumpled on the floor, helpless to stop her. "I'll see you at the theater. But you won't see me. Neither will anyone else."

CHAPTER 14

Ring! Ring!

Clark groaned. On the nightstand, Dawn's telephone jangled again. Someone had been calling incessantly, but Clark couldn't make it across the room to answer it. Each ring felt like a lava arrow shooting through his skull. The pain was nearly blinding, sending him to the brink of an inky abyss.

Can't . . . pass out. Have to . . . think.

With all his will, he fought the pain. But the scarlet siren of unconsciousness, and whatever was beyond, lured him with a promise of blessed relief.

No. I won't give . . . in.

Breathing raspily, he forced himself to take

stock of his surroundings. He was on the polished wooden floor of Dawn's room. Shattered pieces of green meteorite were scattered around him. Benign to anyone else, they could kill him, and *would* kill him soon, if he didn't find a way to escape.

On the nightstand, Dawn's phone rang again.

They're calling from the theater, Clark realized. *They must be panicking, with me and Dawn both missing. If only I could reach the phone . . .*

But the phone might as well have been on the moon — he knew he couldn't reach it. He was too weak even to kick the rocks away. Grunting with the effort, he turned his head. Each centimeter of movement sent molten pain shooting down his spinal column. Now he could see his watch. It was 7:30 P.M.

People are arriving at the theater. Dawn is probably there by now. Lana and everyone else are in danger. If I don't get out of here, they're all dead.

What was that? Had he just heard someone downstairs? Clark tried to call out, but only the weakest puff of air escaped his bloodless lips.

Suddenly, Tillie was in the doorway, staring at him. "Hey! What are you doing here?" She paled. "Oh, my gosh, Dawn tried to kill you, right?"

"No. Sprained ankle," he lied. "Help . . . me."

"*That's* all?" The girl rolled her eyes. "Jeez, you're as big of a drama queen as the witch. I've had a sprained ankle, you know. It's not such a big deal."

"Have to get . . . to theater," Clark breathed.

"No sugar, Sherlock. We just stopped home for Dawn's flowers. Dawn makes my parents give her a big bouquet at every curtain call." Tillie leaned contemplatively against the doorframe, considering the possibilities. "Of course, if you're here, the show can't go on, can it? Dawn would totally lose it. That'd be *sweet.*"

"Need you to move those . . ." Clark barely nudged his chin toward the meteorite fragments.

"Hey! That's my rock!" Tillie shrieked. "Who broke my rock? That was one of my best ones!" She scrambled to gather up the green chunks. As she did, Clark felt instantly better.

"Tillie!" an annoyed male voice called from

downstairs. "We're late! How long does it take to go to the bathroom?"

Tillie trotted out of the room and called down to her father. "Daddy! You better get up here. There's a guy in Dawn's room!"

Before Tillie got the word "room" fully out of her mouth, Clark dove out Dawn's still-open window. He did a graceful somersault in the air, looping over the swimming pool before landing on his feet like a cat.

Dawn's parents are going to think that Tillie's making this all up, Clark thought. *But I can't stick around to change their minds. I've got to stop Dawn.*

By the time that thought had fully formed in Clark's mind, he was already a super-speeding blur halfway to Smallville High School.

Chapter 15

"He's here!" Carrie cried, as soon as she saw Clark come through the backstage door. The news spread instantly. Both words of relief and angry accusations followed Clark as he tracked down Mr. Gullet. He found the director near the prop table.

"Do you have any idea what you put your colleagues through by showing up so late?" Mr. Gullet thundered, his eyes stormy. Clark opened his mouth to reply, but the director held his palm up to silence him. "Never mind, I don't want to hear it. Get into costume. Have you seen Miss Mills?"

Clark hesitated. What could he say? That Dawn had found a way to make herself invisible but now she couldn't reverse it? That she'd attacked her friends and tried to kill Lana? That she was probably at the theater that very moment, bent on murderous revenge, but her invisibility would make it impossible to stop her? That no one was safe and they should cancel the show?

"Mr. Kent?" Mr. Gullet prompted. "In this lifetime?"

If I say all that, they'll think I'm crazy, because I'll sound crazy, Clark realized. *They won't stop the show. They'll just stop me from stopping Dawn.*

There was only one thing to do.

"Mr. Gullet, I —" Clark began.

"Clark!" Lana ran to him, clad in Dawn's first-act costume, a *Cyrano* script in her hand. "I *knew* you wouldn't let everyone down. Chloe told me you went to look for Dawn," she rushed on. "Mr. Gullet asked me to go on as Roxanne if she doesn't show up. Did you find her?"

"The exact question I was just asking," Mr. Gullet put in impatiently.

"I didn't . . . *see* her," Clark said carefully. He knew he had to get out of there — that every moment's delay tipped the odds further in Dawn's favor.

The director turned to Lana. "In that case, Lana, you are Roxanne."

Lana went gray. "Serves me right for knowing the lines better than anyone else." She gulped hard, then tried to rally. "Well, I admit it, I'm petrified. But if I'm about to make my unscheduled theatrical debut, I'm glad it'll be with you, Clark."

How could this be happening? It was bad enough that everyone in the show, as well as the audience, would know that Clark Kent had ruined the school play. Let everyone down. Chickened out. But now, he was also turning down the chance to be Lana's leading man?

From outside, Clark heard a rumble of thunder. The weather must have turned. Well, that certainly fit his mood. He turned to the director. "I'm sorry, Mr. Gullet. I know you won't understand, but . . . I can't go on."

"What do you mean, you can't go on?" the director bellowed angrily. "Of course you're going on. Everyone is counting on you!"

"I'm sorry, sir. I can't."

The director was livid. Lana was stunned. But he couldn't let himself think about that now. His mind was already on Dawn. What would she do? What might she already have done?

"You have terminal stage fright, Mr. Kent?" Mr. Gullet asked, his tone withering.

"Something like that, sir." Clark's eyes flicked up to the catwalk, where a heavy light wobbled, as if the bolts that held it had been loosened. Was it Dawn? He had to get up there. He turned to Lana. "I wish I could explain."

Her disappointment was written on her face. "I wish you could, too, Clark."

God, why did it have to be this way? How he longed to assure her that he wasn't the loser he appeared to be, to dazzle her with the brilliance of his Cyrano, and to bow hand in hand with her to thunderous applause.

But it was not to be.

"I'm so sorry," he told her softly. "I have to go."

ꕥ ꕥ ꕥ ꕥ

Accompanied by the excited voices of the audience and the percussion of rain on the roof above, Clark crawled along the catwalk, high above the still-empty stage. He reached the massive steel lighting fixture and checked the bolts. Sure enough, they were loose. He quickly tightened them with his bare hands, wondering if Dawn was watching him at that very moment.

"Dawn?" he whispered. "Please listen to me. I know you don't really want to hurt these people. Dawn?"

There was no answer. Down below, Clark saw Carrie run frantically across the stage. Were they going to cancel the performance? No, Mr. Gullet would probably go on as Cyrano. Clark quickly X-rayed through the curtain and out into the audience. There were his parents. His mom wore her best black dress. His dad, who lived in jeans and flannel shirts, had on a sports jacket. They looked so excited and proud. They'd be so . . .

Clark tore his eyes away and went back to business. They'd understand, once he explained. But they'd be the only ones who would. He checked the heavy canvas flats stretched across wooden supports that would later be lowered to the stage as backdrops. They were held in place by sandbag counterweights and ropes. Clark examined the ropes, not surprised to find they'd been deliberately frayed to the breaking point. If they snapped, it would send the massive sandbags hurling to the stage; death from above for anyone below.

Clark quickly tied knots over the frayed part of each rope.

The house lights were lowered and the audience hushed. Clark saw actors taking their places on stage: guardsmen, soldiers, and townspeople. The curtain went up to reveal a bustling town square, people gossiping about the dueling skill of the famous Cyrano and the unequaled beauty of the fair Roxanne.

Where's Dawn?

He followed the catwalk upstage, until it ended. He blasted his X-ray vision downward to see that he was directly above the scene-and-costume shop. Now that the play had begun, it was deserted.

Wait a minute. Near the back of the shop, a

woodworking lathe was whirring away. The harmless swords that Cyrano and his men would use later in the play were lined up near the lathe. Suddenly, Clark saw one of the swords float through the air until its tip sparked against the whirring lathe.

Dawn.

She was turning the harmless prop swords into killing weapons.

Clark leapt high, then plunged downward, smashing both feet through the shop ceiling. He landed on a work table twenty feet from the lathe. "Give it up, Dawn," he called. "It's over."

Dawn's voice came out of the emptiness. "Nice entrance, cheesy dialogue. Say, shouldn't you be onstage by now? Better hurry, you'll miss your entrance. Lah-na will be *so* miffed."

Suddenly, one of the sharpened swords rocketed at Clark's head. With one dazzling move, he plucked it out of the air. By the razor-sharp tip of the blade.

"What the . . . How the hell did you do that?" Dawn sputtered.

Clark took a huge jump from the table and landed in front of the door to the shop. There were no windows in the room. If he stayed between Dawn and that door, he could stop her from getting out. "I'm not going to let you hurt anyone, Dawn."

She laughed. "You really do need a new writer, Clark. No one actually talks like that."

"I'm serious, Dawn. You're not getting out of here."

"Don't you get it?" Dawn pleaded, her voice softer now. "No one will ever look at me again."

"I'm sure there are doctors who can help you," Clark insisted.

"No one can help me. I'm going to be alone forever. Of all the people who broke my heart, Clark, you know who hurt me the most? You."

Near the sound of her voice, a pneumatic nail-gun floated into the air. Clark knew it was used to drive nails into wood and was far more powerful than a hammer.

"Don't —" Clark began.

"Shut up!" Dawn screamed. The nail-gun

floated closer, spitting deadly projectiles at Clark. The nails pinged off him — chest, arms, face — and fell harmlessly to the floor.

"What's going on?" Dawn screamed. She grabbed a welding torch and ignited the propane — all Clark could see was a hot blue flame licking at the air. It came closer. While Clark knew that he wouldn't burn, his clothing would. And there was so much flammable stuff here in the shop. If it ignited, and the fire spread to the crowded theater . . .

Out of the corner of his eyes, Clark saw something to his left, hanging on the wall. He reached behind him, feeling for the metal doorknob. He grabbed it, and in one swift motion flung it powerfully toward that wall.

If my aim is good . . .

It was good. The improvised brass missile crashed into the big portable fire extinguisher that Clark had seen. The power of the impact blew open the extinguisher's metal capsule — the compressed foam inside it exploded with concussive force, spewing forth in a perfect line, directly at Dawn.

As the jet hit her, it splattered all over her body, up and down, outlining Dawn in a weird foamy silhouette. Finally, she was visible.

"Arrgh! What did you do? It's in my eyes!" Dawn bellowed. Clark grabbed a drop cloth and dove at her, wrapping her in the canvas and pinning her to the ground.

It was over.

CHAPTER 16

Clark stood under an overhang in front of the school, as paramedics slid Dawn into an ambulance. He raised his voice over the pounding rain. "She going to be okay?"

"Her vitals are fine," a paramedic assured Clark, closing the rear of the ambulance. Rain splattered off his yellow slicker. "Thanks for calling, kid. We'll take good care of her. Promise." He trotted around the ambulance, got in, and drove away. Clark watched the flashing lights disappear into the murky night.

For a moment, he held his ground, wondering how he'd ever be able to face Lana, or anyone else at school again. Lana. Maybe he could catch her in the end of the play. At least that would be something.

He hurried back to the theater and slipped inside, standing alone in the rear. Lana was onstage, clad in Roxanne's final costume, an unadorned white gown. Her raven hair was plaited in a simple braid that hung down her back. She took Clark's breath away.

"'When I look at you,'" he whispered, "'I feel as if I can bring the stars down from the heavens.'"

It was the convent scene, near the show's conclusion. Soon, Cyrano would enter, mortally wounded but hiding his injury from his beloved Roxanne. At last, she would realize that it was Cyrano all along who loved her, and that she loved him, too.

A nun entered. "M'lady," she announced to Roxanne. "A gentleman has come to see you."

"Let him come," Roxanne replied.

And now from stage right, Mr. Gullet will enter as Cyrano.

Cyrano entered, walking slowly, weakened by the battle wound he was trying to conceal. Only it wasn't Mr. Gullet. It was Whitney.

Whitney?

"'Fair Roxanne.'" Whitney kissed Lana's hand.

"'Cyrano.'" Lana said the name as a caress.

"Clark."

Clark turned, as a hand touched his shoulder. It was Lex.

"You must have a hell of a story to tell," Lex murmured. "Mr. Gullet informed me at intermission that you had 'flaked out.' That's a direct quote. Somehow I have a feeling it's not the real story."

Clark pointed toward the stage. "How did Whitney —?"

"Part two of the Gullet report has it that the quarterback memorized Cyrano's part without telling anyone. Couldn't have Lana thinking you were one up on him, I suppose. Sort of a theatrical pissing contest."

Clark shook his head. Lex studied his friend in the shadowy darkness. "So, Clark. When do I get to hear the real reason you aren't up there?"

"Probably never."

Lex smiled. "For what it's worth, Whitney was awful. He lacks the soul for Cyrano."

"Thanks," Clark managed.

The two of them watched the play's final moments, as Lana cupped her hand gently to Whitney's cheek. "'How could I have been so blind for so long? It was you who loved me all along, Cyrano.'"

"'Yes, always,'" Whitney replied. "'And I will love you until the day I die.'"

Just as Dawn had in dress rehearsal, Whitney disregarded Mr. Gullet's end-of-the-play blocking. He took Lana into his arms and kissed her. As the curtain plummeted, so did Clark's heart. The audience broke into thunderous applause. The curtain rose again, the cast in place for their bows. Center stage, hand in hand, were Lana and Whitney. Together, they took a second bow. The rest of the cast applauded them, too.

"Bravo!" The crowd cheered, rising as one to its feet. "Bravo!"

He didn't need to see anymore. Leaving a curious Lex behind, Clark wordlessly exited the theater. He strode through the empty school hallways and pushed out into the soggy night.

Was this his destiny, to never hear applause ring out for him? Would he spend his life saving lives, only to end up always and forever alone?

"Clark!"

It was his father, calling from the open window of their pickup truck as it rolled to a stop near him. Martha sat next to Jonathan, gazing with concern at her son.

"Hey," Clark said. "Guess you left the play early. Wasn't what you expected, huh?"

"I don't know what happened tonight, Clark," his father said, "but I do know my son. Whatever the reason was that you weren't up there, it had nothing to do with you, and everything to do with something you had to do."

Clark nodded, hardly able to swallow around the lump in his throat.

His mom leaned toward the open window. "You okay, Clark?"

"Yeah," he said. "Now."

Jonathan smiled. "Hop in, son." Martha opened the door on her side for Clark.

"I think I need to walk, Dad."

His father hesitated, until Clark saw Martha put a hand on his arm. "That's fine, Clark," she said.

Jonathan nodded. "We'll see you at home."

The truck pulled away. As it did, the rain intensified anew. Clark zipped up his jacket. The storm lashed his spirit but could not lash his soul, as he walked on into the night.

About the Authors

Cherie Bennett and Jeff Gottesfeld are a well-known writing couple, authors of several award-winning novels for young adults. Cherie is also one of the nation's leading playwrights for teens, a two-time winner of the Kennedy Center's "New Visions/New Voices" award. As part of the inaugural writing staff for *Smallville,* they wrote the first season episode, "Jitters." They answer all their email personally; learn more about them at their Web site, cheriebennett.com.